"Go to bed, Alice."

"Should I make some coffee?"

"Go to your room!" Cameron thundered.

Alice didn't waste a moment. She ran as if the hounds of hell were nipping at her heels. But it wasn't the hounds of hell she feared, it was the devil in blue jeans, the devil named Cameron.

He wanted her. She'd seen it in his eyes, felt it in his touch. He wanted her, and, God help her, she wanted him.

Would he come to her? Would he sneak into her room, make his way through the moonlight that filtered through her window?

She trembled at the thought. The quiver in her body was not a result of fear, but of something much more intense....

Dear Reader,

Happy New Year! And welcome to another month of great reading from Silhouette Intimate Moments, just perfect for sitting back after the hectic holidays. You'll love Marilyn Pappano's *Murphy's Law,* a MEN IN BLUE title set in New Orleans, with all that city's trademark steam. You'll remember Jack Murphy and Evie DesJardiens long after you put down this book, I promise you.

We've got some great miniseries titles this month, too. Welcome back to Carla Cassidy's Western town of MUSTANG, MONTANA in *Code Name: Cowboy.* Then pay a visit to Margaret Watson's CAMERON, UTAH in *Cowboy with a Badge.* And of course, don't forget our other titles this month. Look for *Dangerous To Love,* by Sally Tyler Hayes, a book whose title I personally find irresistible. And we've got books from a couple of our newest stars, too. Jill Shalvis checks in with *Long-Lost Mom,* and Virginia Kantra pens our FAMILIES ARE FOREVER title, *The Passion of Patrick MacNeill.*

Enjoy them all—and be sure to come back next month for more of the most exciting romantic reading around, right here in Silhouette Intimate Moments.

Yours,

Leslie J. Wainger
Executive Senior Editor

Please address questions and book requests to:
Silhouette Reader Service
U.S.: 3010 Walden Ave., P.O. Box 1325, Buffalo, NY 14269
Canadian: P.O. Box 609, Fort Erie, Ont. L2A 5X3

CODE NAME:
COWBOY

CARLA
CASSIDY

Silhouette®

INTIMATE™ MOMENTS®

Published by Silhouette Books

America's Publisher of Contemporary Romance

SILHOUETTE BOOKS

ISBN 0-373-07902-8

CODE NAME: COWBOY

Copyright © 1999 by Carla Bracale

CARLA CASSIDY

is an award-winning author who has written over thirty books for Silhouette. In 1995 she won Best Silhouette Romance of 1995 from *Romantic Times Magazine* for her Silhouette Romance novel *Anything for Danny*. In 1998 she also won a Career Achievement Award for Best Innovative series from *Romantic Times Magazine*.

Carla believes the only thing better than curling up with a good book to read is sitting down at the computer with a good story to write. She's looking forward to writing many more books and bringing hours of pleasure to her readers.

To Mike, a bounty hunter who
shows hero potential!

Chapter 1

Cameron Gallagher had just sat down for lunch when somebody knocked on his front door. He rarely had visitors. His sister, Elena, and her husband and baby were the only ones who came to visit him regularly and he knew they had driven into Billings for the day.

Maybe it was somebody about the housekeeper job. God, he hoped so. The house was a wreck. Not only did the walls need repainting and some Sheetrock patching, the clutter was knee-deep. He'd spent most of his time in the past couple of months getting ready for winter. The inside of the house hadn't been a priority.

When he opened the door, he looked into a pair of eyes so blue he felt as if he'd been punched in the gut.

"Uh...Mr. Gallagher? Cameron Gallagher?"

The sound of her voice, low and melodic, pulled him from his initial shock. He nodded curtly as his eyes traveled the length of her.

She was a small thing…he'd guess just a smidgin over five feet. She looked like a strong gust of wind would take her feet out from beneath her. She was far too thin, with hollow cheeks and dark circles under her eyes. Dark hair framed her face, badly cut and too dark for her complexion.

"I've come about the job." She held out the flyer Cameron had posted the week before in Stella's Diner, the local café.

He figured she'd get one look at the inside of the house and run for the hills. Which was just as good. He didn't know a thing about her, didn't even know her name, but he knew in an instant he didn't want her working for him.

He opened the door to allow her entry. "Come in."

She hesitated only an instant, then stepped inside. As her gaze swept through the living room, he thought he saw her flinch in dismay. He strode over to a chair and moved a pile of papers to the floor. "Have a seat."

Gingerly she walked across the room. Cameron noted that her jeans were designer and her sweater appeared to be genuine cashmere. Not exactly housekeeper attire.

"You're new to Mustang, Ms.…?"

"Alice…Alice Burwell."

Her eyes did not meet his and she seemed uncomfortable.

"Yes, I'm new here," she continued. She cleared her throat and looked directly at him. "I'm a hard worker, Mr. Gallagher, and I really need this job."

She offered him a shy smile and again he felt as if he'd been kicked in the stomach by a mule. The smile lit her features, transformed her from plain to pretty. Definitely not what he had in mind. "I'm looking for a live-in housekeeper," he explained. "I'm looking for somebody who can handle hard work and long winters of isolation. I need somebody who can occasionally rustle up a meal for a gang of rowdy ranch hands and keep her nose out of my personal business."

Her blue eyes turned frosty. "I'm stronger than I look. I like winter months, and I can't imagine I'd be interested in your personal business."

Her spunky response renewed his inexplicable urge to get her out of his house. "Look, Ms. Burwell, you just aren't right for the job." Cam didn't try to hide his impatience. He strode to the door and opened it. "Good luck finding something else," he said, although he knew his tone was too abrupt for any genuine well-wishing.

She stood, her straight back giving her the illusion of additional height. "I see. I appreciate your time." Her tone was curt as well, although he sensed an underlying despair. "Goodbye, Mr. Gallagher."

He closed the door, but moved to the window and watched as she walked toward her car. He tried not to feel responsible for the slump of her shoulders, the defeat she emanated with her bowed head.

He continued watching as she reached her car,

peered inside, then straightened and looked around. What was she doing? Suddenly she headed toward the large tree in the front yard.

The tree held the remnants of an ancient tree house. Cameron had been meaning to pull the old boards and plywood out of the branches, but hadn't done so yet.

Alice stood at the base of the tree, peering upward. What in the hell was she doing? Deciding he needed to find out, he left the window and headed toward the door. Stepping out onto the porch, he heard Alice calling to somebody who was up in the tree.

"Come down, honey. You promised you'd stay in the car, and that tree house doesn't look safe."

Cameron walked over to where Alice stood. Her cheeks flamed pink as she saw him. "Rebecca, get down right now."

As Cameron looked up, a tiny head peered down over the side of the rickety platform. With huge blue eyes and pixie features, she looked like a little elf.

"Mommy, if we put a roof on it, we could live here," she said.

Alice's cheeks flamed brighter. "Rebecca, I'm not going to tell you again. Come down from that tree house."

"I can't." The two words held a tremble of fear.

"Going up is always easier than coming down," Cameron said, suddenly behind her. "I'll help her down." Without waiting for a response, he grabbed the massive tree trunk and hoisted himself up by using the natural footholds that had made the tree perfect for climbing.

When he reached the platform, he peered over it to see a tiny sprite of a girl sitting in the center. She eyed him suspiciously.

"If you'll come closer, you can wrap your arms around my neck and I'll help you get down," Cameron said.

Like her mother, the little girl had dark shadows beneath her eyes, shadows that gave her a look of haunted vulnerability. And in the depths of those eyes, he saw a sadness too deep, too profound for a child no bigger than a minute.

"Rebecca, let Mr. Gallagher help you down," Alice instructed from the ground below.

"Are you Mr. Lallager?" Rebecca asked.

"That's me."

"Are you a cowboy?"

Cameron had been called many things in his life, most which shouldn't be repeated for innocent ears. "I ride horses...and most of the time I wear a cowboy hat."

She eyed him for a long moment, as if weighing his character with eyes too wise for her tender age. "Okay," she finally agreed. She scooted on her bottom over to him and wrapped her arms around his neck.

She smelled of childhood innocence, sweet dreams and sunshine. Cameron felt the scent flood through him and he steeled himself against it. She clung to him trustingly as he carried her back to safety. He deposited her next to her mother.

"Mommy, I like it here. There's horses in the back and a swing, and the tree house and everything. Are we going to stay here, Mommy, or do we have to sleep in the car again? I got my fingers crossed so we can stay here." She held up her hand to show them her crossed fingers.

Sleep in the car? Cameron gazed at Alice curiously, then looked at the car. The four-door sedan was old, rusted around the tire wells and the front windshield had a crack that ran from the passenger side to the center. They'd been sleeping in the car?

"Only for the past two nights," she said as if reading his mind.

"Things are that bad?" he asked, although he really didn't want to know. He didn't want to be drawn into this woman's problems.

She shrugged, her shoulders once again stiff with pride. "I told you I needed a job. We're a bit down on our luck. But we'll be fine. Come on, Rebecca. We'll go back into town and see if we can't find something there." She took her daughter's hand and once again started for the car.

As they walked past Cameron, Rebecca looked back over her shoulder at him. Her expression was painfully sad.

How could he send them away, knowing they apparently had no money and no place to go? What would happen to them? Cameron cursed beneath his breath, already regretting what he was about to do. "Come back inside. We'll talk about the terms of the position."

* * *

"I'll show you to your room," Cameron said after they finished a quick discussion about her duties, hours and salary.

Alicia took Rebecca's hand and quickly followed him up the stairs, afraid at any moment he might change his mind.

She had almost turned the car around and left when the house had come into view. There was nothing welcoming about the Gallagher ranch. Dark, weathered wood covered by peeling, gray paint made up the two-story structure. Dark shutters were pulled tight over the upstairs windows, and the front porch had an ominous sag in the center.

But Alicia knew their options were running out, and she was not only bone weary, but soul weary as well. The flyer she'd seen in the local café had indicated the Gallagher ranch was named the Last Hope Ranch.

Last Hope Ranch, indeed. She knew she was nearing the last of her hope...hope for a home, a future. She had to settle someplace for Rebecca. And in the back of her mind, she knew this was the last place on earth anyone would ever think to look for her. If nothing else, that made this job perfect for her.

"It isn't much, but you should be comfortable in here," he said as he opened the door to a midsize bedroom. He flipped on the light, as the sunshine was unable to filter through the tightly shuttered windows.

It was obvious the room wasn't used on a regular basis. A fine layer of dust coated the surface of the double dresser and an ugly, but serviceable brown quilt covered the full-size bed.

"This will be fine," Alicia replied. At least with so little furniture, Rebecca would have room to play with the few toys they'd packed and brought with them.

Cameron strode to the window, opened it, shoved back the shutters, and the flood of golden sunshine softened the starkness of the room. "The girl can sleep in the room next door," he said as he turned and looked at Alicia.

"We don't need to take up two rooms," Alicia protested. "Rebecca will be fine in here with me."

He frowned, the result an expression as unwelcoming as the appearance of the house. "All kids should have their own rooms."

"Oh, yes, Mommy. Please? I want my own room," Rebecca chimed in.

Without waiting for Alicia's reply, Cameron walked to the room next door. In there, he repeated the process of opening the shutters, and the sun played on the hardwood floor of the much smaller room. A single-size bed was against one wall, a chest of drawers on the opposite one. Like the other room, this one looked as if it hadn't been used in months…or years.

Rebecca walked across the room and sat on the edge of the bed. She bounced once…twice. "Yes, this will be a good room." Rebecca gave Cameron the sunny, sweet smile Alicia hadn't seen from her daughter in a very long time.

Cameron's frown seemed to deepen into a genuine scowl. "You can get settled in today and begin work tomorrow. Mornings come early around here. I'm usually up and ready for breakfast by five-thirty."

Before she could respond, he turned and left the room. His footsteps thundered down the stairs and Alicia released the breath she hadn't realized she'd been holding.

Her initial meeting with Cameron Gallagher had prompted a renewed urge in Alicia to turn around and leave. The appearance of the house had been unwelcoming, Cameron Gallagher had appeared positively forbidding.

Her first impression had been of a man made up of varying degrees of darkness. Ebony hair...midnight eyes...the deep shadow of whiskers across his lower jaw. Darkness...with no hint of light anywhere to be found.

"It's a good room, isn't it, Mommy?" Rebecca's voice pulled Alicia from her thoughts. "Almost as good as the one I used to have."

Alicia looked around, trying to still the ache in her heart as she thought of Rebecca's room in their beautiful four-bedroom house in Texas. There, Rebecca had enjoyed a room fit for a fairy princess, with lots of pink ruffles and bows. The fact that Rebecca was so willing to be content in this austere room only told Alicia how little her daughter had come to expect from life.

She walked over and gave Rebecca a hug. "Yes, it's a fine room, although it's very dusty. Why don't I go get some cleaning supplies and we'll clean the two rooms together? Then we'll get our things from the car and move in.''

"Okay." Rebecca hugged Alicia around the waist. "I'm glad I crossed my fingers 'cause I really wanted to live here with the tree house and the horses and the cowboy.''

Alicia laughed. Hope swelled up in her heart. Surely nobody would ever find them here.

It had been the whims of fate that had led them to the dusty little town of Mustang, Montana. Hundreds of miles from their home in Dallas, surely they would be safe here…at least for a little while. It had seemed a stroke of good fortune when they'd lunched at the cozy café and Alicia had spotted the flyer advertising for a housekeeper. Out of money, tired of running, Alicia had taken a chance. Now, time alone would tell if she and Rebecca could be happy here.

She hadn't used her real name, and although she felt bad about lying, she was more afraid of using her real name. It was imperative that she and Rebecca not be found by people in Dallas, imperative they not be found until Alicia had a plan.

She sent a small prayer upward. Let us be safe here…let us be safe at least for a little while.

It took them nearly two hours to dust the furniture and mop the hardwood floors with vinegar and water. Despite the outside chill, Alicia opened the windows to allow in the crisp, fresh-scented air.

By the time they carried their things in from the car, the rooms had begun to take on a more personal aura. Alicia's few toiletries lined the top of the

dresser, the expensive cologne and face cream a reminder of the life she'd left behind. A gilded frame
held a snapshot of Robert, a smiling two-year-old
Rebecca in his arms.

Rebecca's room had taken on the distinct personality of the new occupant. Three favorite stuffed animals occupied a place of honor in the center of the
bed. A small box of dolls and toys was against the
wall beneath the window, and her favorite pastel-
colored blanket draped across the plain brown
corded spread, adding a soft rainbow of girlish colors.

"Now will you push me on the swing that's in
the backyard?" Rebecca asked.

Alicia hesitated, unsure if it was a good idea or
not. Cameron had gone outside as soon as Alicia
had retrieved the cleaning supplies from the kitchen
pantry.

Although it was obvious that Rebecca had been
the trump card that had landed Alicia the job, Alicia
had a feeling Cameron preferred children to be neither seen nor heard. She didn't want to jinx this
opportunity before they took advantage of it. She
needed to work long enough to save up some
money, in case things with Broderick, her father-in-
law, came to a crisis.

"Okay," she finally relented. It was probably a
good idea to let Rebecca spend some time outside
and work off her energy so she would play quietly
this evening. Besides, after the last couple of weeks
cooped up in the car, Alicia knew her daughter
yearned for physical activity.

Alicia zipped Rebecca's jacket, then threw on her own and together mother and daughter headed downstairs. As they walked, Alicia noticed the carved oak bannister and the steps that were dull with old wax. All that was needed to turn the wide staircase into a showpiece was a little elbow grease.

In fact, as they passed through the living room on their way to the front door, she realized much of what had looked so disheartening at first glance, was really just the need for order and cleanliness. Beneath the clutter the wood floors themselves were in good shape. The stone fireplace wasn't chipped or broken. Although the walls needed a little patchwork, a coat of paint would do wonders to improve the appearance.

Alicia wasn't afraid of hard work. She'd spent most of her adolescence taking care of herself. She'd moved out of her parents home at eighteen and had worked as a waitress in a busy truck stop, enduring long hours and backbreaking work. Then she'd met Robert and for a little while she'd felt like Cinderella, saved from a life of toil by the handsome prince. And then the prince had died, and Alicia had been left to deal with his wicked father and mother.

"Come on, Mommy," Rebecca exclaimed impatiently as she tugged Alicia through the front door.

"Race you to the swing," Alicia said.

Rebecca squealed in delight and took off around the side of the house. Alicia followed right behind, laughing as her daughter peered back at her, blue eyes wide with merriment.

As they rounded the edge of the house into the

back, both mother and daughter stopped short. "Oh, Mommy, look at the horse," Rebecca said.

Cameron stood in the center of the large corral, a long rope tied to the reddish-brown horse. Alicia wasn't sure who exactly was in control as man and beast faced each other.

The horse's back legs skittered sideways, then she pawed the ground and snorted angrily. Alicia caught her breath as the horse reared up on hind legs, front hooves slashing the air menacingly.

Cameron's back and arm muscles corded with the effort to hang on to the tether, his features set in grim determination. The horse dropped back to all fours, then shook her head and attempted to back up from Cameron.

"Isn't she pretty?" Rebecca exclaimed.

"Yes," Alicia replied, but it wasn't the horse that held her attention, it was the man.

She couldn't help but notice how his jeans cupped tight around his buttocks and molded to his powerful thighs. His blue flannel shirt strained across broad shoulders. A black hat was pulled down far enough to cast shadows across his eyes...eyes that appeared to be made up solely of dark shadows.

Just beneath the clippety clop of the hooves against the hard ground, Alicia could hear his voice. Although she couldn't make out the words, she knew he was gentling the skittish horse. His tone was deep and smooth, like a hot toddy on a wintry night, and it sent a resulting warmth through Alicia.

Oh, how she wished she had strong arms to hold her, a deep, rich voice to soothe her and tell her everything was going to be all right. How she wished she wasn't so alone in the mess that her life had become.

"Come on, Mommy. Let's swing." Rebecca grabbed Alicia's hand and tugged her toward an old tire swing that dangled from a thick branch of a huge tree.

"Wait," Alicia instructed, wanting to inspect the condition of the branch, the rope and the tire to ensure Rebecca's safety. It took her only a moment to confirm that the branch was strong, the rope unfrayed and the tire good enough to hold Rebecca.

She helped her daughter into the swing and as she pushed Rebecca she found her gaze returning again and again to the man in the corral.

Cameron Gallagher. Darkly handsome. Blatantly sexy. Her new boss. She had a feeling he would be a hard taskmaster. That was okay with her. The harder she worked, the less time she'd have to think about the monsters that chased her. Real monsters who seemed to be omnipotent. She shivered and pulled her jacket closer around her neck.

Surely they wouldn't find her here. Montana was miles away from Texas. Surely she and Rebecca were safe, at least for a little while. Nobody would expect to find Alicia Randall working as a housekeeper on a ramshackle ranch in Montana.

Again her gaze went to Cameron, and she felt a renewed swirl of heat in the pit of her stomach. She recognized it for what it was…instant attraction, a strange combustible reaction. She'd felt it the moment she'd seen him.

It didn't mean anything, and the last thing she needed in her life right now was any kind of a relationship with anyone. She had too many secrets, too much to lose if she divulged those secrets.

She tore her gaze away from her new employer. Sexy. Attractive. And definitely off-limits. She'd do her work, save her money and hope to hell Broderick and his wife didn't find her here until she had come up with a plan to somehow defeat him.

Chapter 2

Cameron's concentration faltered the moment Alice and her daughter rounded the side of the house. Although he continued to work with the horse, his heart was no longer in the job.

He knew Alice Burwell and her daughter being here was a mistake. He didn't like the sound of their laughter as mother pushed daughter on the stupid swing he'd meant to take down months ago.

He didn't like the way Alice's blue eyes reminded him so vividly of Ginny's. Ginny, who'd betrayed him, made a mockery of their love.

Cameron expelled a grunt of disgust. Two years and still anger coursed through him when the memories broke through the wall he tried to keep erected against them.

Knowing it was useless to work the horse any longer, he took the rope from her and allowed her free rein in the corral. She pranced like a show horse, as if proud that she'd won this particular battle of spirit.

As Cameron stepped out of the corral, he saw Burt Winston approaching from the stables. Cameron had hired Burt and a handful of other men a month before. He intended to work the men through the winter mending fencing, salvaging what could be saved of the dilapidated outbuildings. Come spring they would all be too busy with the livestock Cameron intended to buy, but winter was time for repairs.

"Hey, boss, we need a bunch of supplies in order to fix the fences in the west pasture. There's not much that can be salvaged of the old fencing."

Cameron nodded. "Place an order with Johnny down at Hopkins Yard. He'll bill it to me and have it delivered. I'd like that fence mended before the first snow."

Burt frowned and raised his gaze to the clear blue sky overhead. "Don't know if that's possible or not. Doesn't look or feel like snow, but my bones tell me the white stuff is right around the corner."

"I hope your bones are lying because we've still got a lot to get done around here," Cameron said.

Burt eyed Alice and Rebecca curiously. "Visitors?"

"New housekeeper," Cameron replied. "Alice Burwell."

"Burwell. Don't believe I know them." Burt prided himself on knowing every family in a hundred-and-fifty mile radius of Mustang.

"They aren't from around here." Cameron frowned. The lady had told him they were from back east, but he knew a Texas accent when he heard one, and Alice Burwell was definitely a Texas native.

He deepened his frown. He didn't care if the lady was from Venus as long as she could bring order and hot meals to his home. "Get that material ordered today," he said to Burt.

"Will do," Burt replied and with a tip of his hat. He turned and walked back toward the stables where Cameron knew he'd make the call from the phone on the wall outside the horse stalls.

Cameron had a total of six men working for him and living in the bunkhouse, a wooden, one-story structure in the distance. He hoped he'd need to hire a half dozen more come spring. Sooner or later he wanted his ranch not only to be a comfortable home, but also a thriving business.

Time. It would take time. It had taken him ten years working as a bounty hunter to finally get together the money to buy this place. The money he'd inherited upon the death of his parents would help him build his dream ranch.

His inheritance money had been unavailable for some time as the trustee and his sister's first husband had stolen it. The money had since been returned, and justice had prevailed.

His parents would have been proud of his choice to leave behind the bounty hunting business and instead focus on ranching for a living. They'd worried about him. They'd been afraid he'd lose his life as a bounty hunter. But their worry was for naught.

Cameron had been good, too good to be taken down. Unfortunately, nobody had warned him about losing his soul.

He finished chores, checked the horses in the stable and locked up for the night, then headed for the house. The swing in the yard was empty and swayed listlessly in the evening breeze.

He thought of the little girl who now occupied his home...a little girl with corn-silk hair and a sadness in her eyes that somehow had crawled into his heart.

It had been the kid that had made him relent and give Alice the job...even though she looked about as capable of doing heavy housework as he was of performing ballet.

The moment he entered the house, their presence was instantly apparent. The scent of tangy tomato sauce wafted from the kitchen and soft, feminine voices filled up what had always been a comfortable silence.

His stomach growled with hunger pangs. It had been months since he'd had a good, home-cooked meal. Most nights he grabbed a sandwich or zapped a microwave dinner or made the ten-minute drive into town to eat at the café.

He walked into the kitchen and stopped short at the sight that greeted him. Alice stood at the stove, stirring a pot of bubbling spaghetti sauce. Rebecca sat at the table, a book opened in front of her. They both froze at the sight of him. He said nothing although he was oddly irritated by the skittish look in Alice's eyes.

"I know you said I didn't have to start work until

morning, but it seemed silly just to sit up in the bedroom when I could be cleaning down here and cooking something for dinner.''

She turned to her daughter, who stared at Cameron as if she wasn't sure if she should smile...or run. ''Rebecca, you go on up to your room now so Mr. Gallagher can eat his dinner in peace.'' Rebecca closed her book and stood obediently.

''No sense sending her off to her room,'' Cameron said grudgingly. ''Have you two eaten?''

Alice hesitated, then shook her head. ''I figured we'd eat after you're finished.'' She felt her cheeks pinken with a blush. ''It's usually improper for the help to eat with the employer.''

Cameron swept his hat off and hung it on a rack by the backdoor. ''This is Montana, Alice. You'll discover very quickly that people out here don't pay much attention to the rules of proper society.'' He moved over to the sink to wash his hands. ''And you'll discover even quicker that I am one of the worst culprits of all when it comes to breaking rules.''

He washed his hands and dried them, then sat down at the table next to the little girl. ''We'll eat together, and for the record, my name is Cameron, not Mr. Gallagher. Mr. Gallagher was my father, and he's dead.''

He jumped as Rebecca touched his hand. ''Your daddy is dead, too? So is mine.'' Something deep inside Cameron responded to the aching pain in the little girl's eyes. For a split second, he wanted to take her in his arms and hold her until that pain dissipated.

Before he could do anything, Rebecca smiled. "Maybe your daddy and my daddy are friends in Heaven. Wouldn't that be nice?"

"Rebecca, put your book away and set the table for me, please." Alice offered Cameron a smile of apology.

He said nothing, afraid he wouldn't be able to speak around the lump in his throat.

Odd, that a child's innocent words had touched on a hurt Cameron hadn't even been aware existed. Somehow in the multitude of losses he'd suffered in a short amount of time, he'd shoved aside any grieving for his parents.

Rebecca's words suddenly made him yearn for his father's deep voice, the touch of his dry, work-worn hands. He could remember the scent of his mother, a fragrance of fresh-baked bread and lilac talcum powder.

They had died in a plane crash, long before Cameron had been willing to tell them goodbye. He looked at Rebecca, wondering how her father had died, then instantly shoved the curiosity away. He didn't want to know. He didn't want to care.

Within minutes the meal was on the table. Cameron helped himself to a heaping portion of the spaghetti and meatballs. Alice helped Rebecca fill her plate, then her own.

As they ate, the only sound in the kitchen was the rhythmic tick of the clock above the stove and the dull thud of Rebecca's foot kicking the wooden pedestal of the table.

Cameron felt no need to fill the awkward silence. He'd been alone for too long. Silence had become his friend. As he ate, he found his gaze focusing again and again on the woman across the table from him.

She wasn't exactly pretty. She looked tired, almost haggard. He could have given her a better haircut with his sheep shears, and again he noticed the color of her hair was all wrong for her skin tones.

The cashmere sweater she wore was splattered with tomato sauce, but the blue color emphasized the vivid hue of her eyes. Her lashes were long, accentuated with a light touch of mascara.

When she caught him looking at her, she offered him a tentative smile. The gesture transformed plain into pretty and a swirl of heat unfurled in Cameron's stomach.

Damn. He'd been too long alone, too long without a woman. How else to explain the effect of a simple smile on his equilibrium?

Scowling, he looked down at his plate. Hiring Alice was a mistake. Having her and her daughter living in his home was a bigger mistake. But it was difficult to consider firing her as he ate the best spaghetti dinner he'd ever had.

As he finished eating, he was aware of Rebecca's gaze on him. She studied him with the unselfconsciousness of youth, as if trying to decide if she was going to like him or not. "That was a big horse in the corral." She finally spoke.

"Her name is Mischief."

Rebecca giggled. "That's what my mommy calls me sometimes. Miss Mischief."

"Rebecca, stop kicking the table and finish eating," Alice said.

Rebecca did as she was told. The rhythmic thud halted as she scooped a forkful of spaghetti into her mouth. One errant noodle latched onto her chin. "Cowboys love their horses," she said, the noodle dancing with each word, then finally falling back to her plate. "Do you love Mischief?"

"Rebecca, let Mr. Gal…Cameron eat his dinner." Alice smiled at him apologetically. Again that smile of hers carried a punch and filled him with irritation.

He finished eating and shoved back from the table, eager to escape Alice Burwell and her winsome smile. "I'll be in the office next to the living room if you need anything."

The office had originally been meant to be a formal dining area, but Cameron had taken over the space as an office/den. It was the first room of the house he'd completely redone. He'd painted the walls, installed floor-to-ceiling bookshelves and a rich oak desk where he worked most nights on the ranch books.

He settled in at his desk and leaned back, trying to block out the sounds coming from the kitchen. Feminine sounds. Family sounds. They reminded him of old dreams long abandoned. He hated them.

He worked long after the noises from the kitchen had stopped and the house had grown dark and silent. It was after eleven when he finally closed the books and left the office, eager for a hot shower and the comfort of his king-size mattress.

In the bathroom he found evidence of his new housemates. The scent of strawberry bubble bath greeted him. A bottle of the stuff sat on the edge of the tub, contained in a decanter shaped like a smiling, friendly spotted dog.

Beneath the scent of strawberries, he could smell Alice…the slightly spicy, mysterious scent he'd noticed before. He hadn't considered the ramifications of sharing a bathroom.

As he picked up the soap and lathered himself, his mind instantly conjured up an image of his new housekeeper doing the same. He could easily imagine Alice with her head thrown back as she smoothed the soap across her breasts, over her slender torso and down…he plunged his head beneath the spray as he grabbed the faucet for more cold water.

His sister, Elena, had been trying to fix him up with every single woman in town for the past month. Maybe it was time he take her up on the offers. Man was not made to live alone, without the comfort of an occasional roll in the hay.

He certainly didn't want an emotional commitment of any kind…just a lusty release of animal instincts with a woman who knew his rules. No commitment. No promises. He'd been there…done that…and never intended to do it again.

He stepped out of the shower and grabbed a towel. He dried off, then wrapped the towel around his waist and peered into the mirror. An unsmiling face reflected back at him. An unsmiling face desperately in need of a shave. He lathered efficiently, wishing he were one of those men who only had to shave once every couple of days.

He placed the shaving cream back in the medicine cabinet and quickly and methodically shaved. He placed his razor back on the medicine cabinet shelf, then sluiced his face with cold water.

A scream split the silence of the night.

Cameron jumped and tore from the bathroom. He collided in the hallway with Alice, her palms hitting his chest, his hands grabbing her shoulders.

In the spill of light from the bathroom, she looked like a wide-eyed wraith in a floor-length white silk nightgown that revealed rather than concealed her figure. Her skin was warm and soft beneath his hands. Too warm. Too soft. He released her at the same time she pulled back her hands from him as if burned.

Another scream pierced the air and a renewed burst of adrenaline fired through Cameron. "She's having a nightmare," Alice said as she flew past him and into Rebecca's room.

"It's all right, sweetie. Mommy is here."

Cameron stood outside the bedroom, listening to the sounds of mother soothing daughter. Choked sobs came from Rebecca, but she quieted quickly beneath the calming voice and touch of her mother. The adrenaline that had shot through him at the scream slowly ebbed away.

He glanced into the room. A night-light burned in

a wall socket, illuminating the area around the bed. Alice sat on the edge of the bed, her daughter wrapped in her arms. She rocked back and forth, her lips whispering softly into Rebecca's ear.

She looked up and saw him. Gently, she placed Rebecca back beneath the blankets and joined him in the hallway. "I apologize. Sometimes she has bad dreams." She frowned worriedly. "I can't promise it won't happen again."

"Nobody can control bad dreams." Cameron knew all about nightmares. They were unwelcome, but familiar visitors to his sleep.

"She should sleep the rest of the night through. When she has the nightmare, it usually only comes once that night."

He nodded, trying not to notice how her breasts thrust against the silk material, how the pale gown did little to hide the rosy circles that surrounded her nipples.

Her gaze swept down the length of him and her cheeks reddened. The intimacy of their near-nakedness suddenly slapped Cameron upside the head. His bare skin prickled in answer to her gaze and he felt himself responding as if she'd reached out and touched him.

When she looked up at him, her eyes had darkened and the color in her cheeks intensified.

"I'm sorry we bothered you," she mumbled as she backed away from him and toward her bedroom. "Good night." She whirled around and disappeared into her room.

Air expelled from Cameron's lungs on a sigh of

renewed irritation. He entered his own bedroom and closed the door, as if the wooden barrier could bar all thoughts of her as well.

Damn, but her skin had been warm, soft and sweetly scented. He'd nearly forgotten the scent of a woman, the feel of female flesh. He cursed beneath his breath, shoving her mental image away.

He shut off his light, dropped the towel by the side of his bed and crawled in beneath the blankets. What in the hell could a six-year-old have nightmares about? Rebecca should be dreaming of sugarplums and fairies, of sunshine and laughter. What would possibly cause a little girl to scream in such terror in the middle of the night?

He didn't want to know.

He didn't want to know anything about Alice Burwell and her daughter. All he wanted from Alice was a clean house and warm meals.

He didn't want to feel desire or passion. Those emotions always got mixed up inside him with rage. And he didn't want rage back in his life. He'd finally let it go, healed some of the wounds that had nearly destroyed him.

Tomorrow he'd figure out exactly how to deal with Alice Burwell on a strictly nonpersonal level. He'd either figure it out...or he'd fire her.

Chapter 3

A broad chest sprinkled with dark curly hairs. Warm skin covered sinewy muscles that grew taut beneath her fingertips. A towel slung low beneath a lean stomach…a towel clinging to slender hips.

Alicia's heart pounded rapidly as she reached out to untuck the towel from around his waist and as the towel slid to the floor, she woke up. She remained unmoving for a long moment, the erotic dream sending crashing waves of heat through her body.

She knew whose chest it had been, remembered vividly how he had looked in the semidarkness of the hallway, the white towel stark against his dark skin. She remained still for another moment, waiting for her heartbeat to slow to a more normal pace.

Feeling more in control, she rolled over and turned off the alarm, scant seconds before it was to ring. Her room was still dark. Even the sun wasn't up at quarter to five.

Despite the disturbing dream, she felt surprisingly well rested when she pulled herself from the warm bed. At least she hadn't dreamed of Broderick. Too many nights her sleep had been haunted with night-mares of her father-in-law stealing her daughter away from her.

After dressing, she went into the bathroom, where she knew Cameron had recently been. The room smelled of freshly used soap and shaving cream, a masculine scent that stirred memories of her days of marriage to Robert.

As she looked in the mirror, a stranger returned her gaze. She raised her brush to hair that didn't belong to her. She'd cut and dyed it in an effort to make it more difficult for Broderick or any of his minions to find her.

She looked nothing like the pale blond Dallas so-ciety darling she'd once been. She wasn't that woman any longer. She was now a housekeeper to a handsome man who'd stepped into her dreams.

Foolishness. It had been that moment of forced intimacy in the hall the night before that had prompted the silly dream.

Leaving the bathroom she made a mental note to always keep her robe at the foot of the bed. She didn't want to be caught again in the hallway half-naked beneath Cameron Gallagher's dark gaze.

In the kitchen, she started a pot of coffee and got busy preparing breakfast. Within minutes the deli-cious scent of sausage filled the room. With the sausage browned and biscuits in the oven, Alicia poured herself a cup of coffee and sank into a chair at the table.

Rebecca rarely got up before seven-thirty or eight. After Cameron's breakfast, Alicia would start scrubbing down the kitchen. She'd started cleaning in here the night before when she'd made supper, but there was still plenty to be done.

The physical activity of scrubbing and polishing would be good for her. It would keep her thoughts away from Broderick, away from the threat he and his wife posed to her. Hopefully for just a little while she'd forget that Broderick and Ruth wanted her daughter, and had the money and the power to possibly achieve such a goal.

It would also use up some of the restless energy that filled her each time she thought of Cameron.

She frowned. She needed to find out about school for Rebecca. It was important that Rebecca get started as soon as possible so she didn't fall too far behind.

Cameron appeared in the doorway, startling Alicia who jumped out of the chair. "Sit...relax," he commanded. She sat back down as he poured himself a cup of coffee, then joined her at the table.

Tension rippled through her as he eyed her curiously. "Did you sleep well?"

"Fine. Thank you." She frowned and wrapped her fingers around her cup. "I'm sorry we disturbed you last night."

He waved a hand dismissively and took a sip of his coffee, his eyes lingering on her curiously. He frowned, looked down at his cup, then back at her, the curiosity more intense. "When did your husband pass away?" he asked, the abruptness of the personal question startling her.

"A year ago." The tension inside her grew. She hoped he didn't plan on digging too deeply into her life. There were things she couldn't tell him...couldn't tell anyone. She would do nothing to place herself and Rebecca at risk.

"Is that when your daughter started having nightmares?"

Alicia nodded. "We've had a difficult time. His death was unexpected, and we weren't prepared financially for anything like that happening."

"No life insurance?"

She shook her head, unable to actually verbalize the lie.

"No family to help you out?"

Again she shook her head, piling lie upon lie with the gesture. "None. My husband was an adopted, only child, and I'm estranged from my mother and father."

He eyed her curiously, but didn't pursue the topic. "What brought you to Mustang?"

His eyes were so intent...as if he saw through her and recognized her lies. She felt the pink of a blush staining her cheeks. "Cowboys," she answered, pleased that at least this was partially true. "Rebecca wanted to go where there were cowboys. Montana seemed the place to come."

She hesitated a moment, then added to her web of lies. "We had no particular place to go.... Mustang seemed as good a town as any in which to start over.''

His gaze was still far too curious for her comfort. ''Starting over…most people just continue with their lives. They don't usually feel the need to start over.''

She shrugged with forced nonchalance. ''We did.''

He grunted, a noncommittal noise that gave away nothing of his thoughts. He took another sip of his coffee and she breathed a sigh of relief as his gaze slid away from her.

''So, what exactly makes your daughter have nightmares?''

Alicia blinked at the unexpectedness of the question. ''Who knows?'' She forced a light laugh. ''She misses her father. I don't know…all children have nightmares.'' She stood and checked the biscuits in the oven. Seeing they were browned, she pulled them out and set them on the counter. ''You ready for breakfast?''

''Sure.''

It took her only minutes to fry eggs, add the sausage and biscuits to his plate and set it in front of him. As he ate, she scrubbed down the stove top, her gaze constantly drawn to him.

Rebecca would be pleased with the way he looked this morning. Clad in a pair of worn jeans, a pair of scuffed boots and a worn denim shirt, he looked every inch a cowboy. All he lacked was his hat, which she knew he'd toss on his head as he walked out the door to do morning chores.

She waited until he was finished eating before asking him about the local grade school. "You said I will have Wednesdays and Sundays off. I thought I'd see about enrolling Rebecca in school on Wednesday," she said.

"Take this afternoon and get it done. No sense in putting it off a couple of days. Mustang only has two schools. One for kindergarten through eighth grade and the other for nine through twelve."

"Thank you. If I'm off this afternoon to take care of it, I'll work on Wednesday to make up for the time."

"Fine." Again his eyes played on her intently, as if he wanted to ask her something…tell her something. Abruptly he shoved away from the table and stood. "I've got chores to attend to." His tone was curt, clipped, as if he blamed her for somehow keeping him from his morning tasks. "I'll be back around noon for lunch." He grabbed his hat, placed it strategically on his head and left through the backdoor.

Alicia's breath seeped out of her, an escape of pent-up anxiety. She had no idea exactly what it was about him that made her feel so tightly wound. Maybe it was the intensity of his dark eyes…or the blatant sensuality he exuded seemingly without self-awareness.

Despite the fact she'd been married and had borne a daughter, Alicia was a stranger to lust. Although when she'd married Robert years ago, she'd believed herself to be desperately in love with him, in the last several months since his death, and in the process of her grieving, she'd recognized that her supposed love for Robert had been something else altogether.

Irritated by the thoughts taking her back to the past, more aggravated with her crazy feelings where her new employer was concerned, Alicia grabbed Cameron's plate off the table and carried it to the sink.

As she cleaned up the mess, she thought of that moment in the hallway last night. Cameron's gaze had drifted down the length of her and in his eyes she thought she saw a spark of hunger. It had terrified her.

She wasn't even sure she liked the man and yet his gaze had the power to shoot desire through her veins. Maybe this job wasn't such a good idea after all.

While she waited for Rebecca to wake up, Alicia wandered around the house, making mental notes of what needed to be done where. There wasn't a room in the house that didn't need a good dusting and floor scrubbing. Cobwebs hung in corners, windows begged for an ammonia wash and curtains hung limp and dusty from neglect.

She easily found Cameron's bedroom down the hall from her own. His bed was unmade and the area retained the evocative scent of him. The room was devoid of personal items other than a row of toiletries on the top of the dresser. It held no more personality than the spare room he'd given to Alicia.

No family photos, no mementoes from a lover or an ex-wife, there was nothing to attest to what kind of man he was. Odd. Alicia, in her desperate flee from her home, had managed to grab a few personal items that had little monetary value but enormous sentimentality.

She'd just finished making Cameron's bed and dusting his room when Rebecca appeared in the doorway. Clad in a long green nightgown, her eyelids still droopy with sleep, she looked like a little elf just awakened from a catnap.

"Good morning, sweetheart," Alicia said as she stepped out of Cameron's bedroom and pulled her daughter into her arms.

"Mornin'," Rebecca replied as she rubbed one eye with a closed fist. "I woke up and didn't know where we were. Then I remembered we were here with Mr. Lallager and the swing and the horses and the tree house." She gave her mother a sweet smile. "Can I go outside and play?"

Alicia shook her head. "First, breakfast. Then we'll see about playing outside." Alicia's heart expanded as she saw Rebecca's enthusiasm…a trait that had been ominously absent in the child for the last several months.

"How about a big bowl of oatmeal?" Alicia suggested as they walked down the stairs toward the kitchen.

"With raisins?"

"I'll have to see if Mr. Gallagher has any raisins."

There were no raisins to be found in the cupboards, but Rebecca was just as happy with a spoonful of honey added to the hot breakfast cereal.

After eating, Rebecca went up to her room and dressed, then once again asked to go outside. Alicia hesitated before answering. She didn't want Rebecca bothering Cameron, but knew this was probably going to be one of the last nice days left before winter arrived.

Despite the fact that it had somehow been Rebecca who had won the job for her, Cameron didn't appear to be the kind of man who would abide a child's presence and prattle for long.

"Okay," she finally said. "You may go to the swing and play…but no place else. And if you see Mr. Gallagher, don't bother him," she finished sternly.

"I won't," Rebecca agreed, already running for the backdoor. Alicia caught up with her long enough to zip her jacket and give her a kiss on the cheek.

The moment Rebecca flew out the door, Alicia moved to the kitchen window, pleased that from this vantage point she could see the corral and the swing that dangled from the tree. Rebecca appeared, the sun glistening on her pale hair as she clambered into the swing and pumped her little legs to make it move.

As always, Alicia's heart swelled as she gazed at her little girl. No matter what price she had paid, what price she would continue to pay, Rebecca was the best thing that had ever happened to her. The little girl embodied the best of Robert and the best of Alicia.

Satisfied that her daughter was happily occupied for the moment, Alicia got back to work.

* * *

It was difficult to fire a good cook. After all, good food was the way to a man's heart, right? Cameron stood in the barn, eyeing the sagging hayloft, his thoughts on Alice Burwell.

He'd awakened with every intention of telling her she had to go…that she just wasn't what he wanted in a housekeeper. But with the scent of sausage and oven-baked biscuits wafting in the air, and Alice looking so damned eager to please, he hadn't been able to follow through on his plan.

Besides, the idea of her and the kid living in their car bothered him. What kind of man died and left his family so destitute? What kind of life had they had before her husband died? He shoved away these questions, irritated with his sudden burst of curiosity. He hadn't been curious about anything or anyone for a long time and the sudden interest felt alien and unwelcome.

He left the barn, making a mental note to have a couple of the men see what they could do to shore up the loft. Eventually he'd like to use it to store hay for the winter. At the moment his hay bales were stored in the oversize garage.

Outside the morning sun warmed his shoulders as he walked toward the corral. The wild horse snorted as if to protest his appearance. Cameron leaned against the railing, watching the magnificent beast dance within the enclosed space. Her head was held high as her nostrils flared a warning.

In the first few days he'd had her, he'd tried to subdue her with sheer force alone, only to realize her will was as stubborn as his own. He realized now the only way to break her was to gentle her, be patient enough to gain her trust.

"Hi, Mr. Lallager." Rebecca climbed up on the lower rung of the corral fence and gazed up at him with those eyes filled with shadows. "You gonna ride Mischief?"

"She won't let me."

"How come?" Rebecca moved closer, so close he could smell the scent of childhood that lingered on her.

"She's wild. She's never had a person on her back before and she doesn't much like it."

"Where did you get her?"

"I caught her in a box canyon."

Once again she looked up at him, skepticism playing on her gamine features. "You catched her in a box?"

Cameron laughed, surprising himself. His laughter sounded rusty to his own ears. It had been a long time since he'd laughed. "Not a box, a box canyon," he corrected. "It's a narrow valley with high sides and only one way in and out."

Rebecca nodded thoughtfully. "Could you go back there and catch me a horse?"

"Do you know how to ride a horse?"

"No. But you could teach me." She frowned, her gaze studying him. "You could teach me how to ride real fast…so if any monsters came after me I could get away."

Cameron fought the impulse to gather her into his arms, assure her that no monsters would ever catch her. He cleared his throat, swallowing the flare of emotions her words evoked. ''What kind of monsters are after you?''

Her eyes widened…blue pools of childish fear. ''People monsters,'' she whispered, as if to speak too loudly might alert the monsters of her whereabouts. ''People monsters who want to keep you and not let you see your mommy ever, ever again.''

Cameron wondered how in the hell a six-year-old would know about people monsters? Cameron knew all about those kind…the human kind who hid behind the faces of friends, smiled benevolently while twisting a knife deep in your back. His monster even had a name.

Samuel Blankenship.

Partner. Friend. Brother. Cameron and Samuel had shared everything: living quarters, ideals, food, philosophies. Like two brothers, the men had a closeness that had made them work like a single unit, until…

He drew a deep breath, trying to dispel the hurt that filled him as thoughts of Samuel filtered through his head. He didn't want to go back to that place in his past, back to the place where he'd believed he had a best friend named Sam and a sweet lover named Ginny. He didn't want to remember that day of reckoning, when they had betrayed him so completely.

''Rebecca.''

Both Cameron and Rebecca turned at the sound of Alice's voice. She stepped off the back porch and hurried toward them, a frown crinkling the center of her forehead. "I told you not to bother Mr. Gallagher!" she exclaimed, then flashed Cameron a look of apology.

"She's fine," he replied. He didn't mind the kid, it was the mother who somehow disturbed him.

"Yeah, I'm fine," Rebecca echoed. "Mr. Lallagher is gonna teach me how to ride a horse and maybe I can get a hat like his and I'll be a real cowgirl."

"I'm sure Mr. Gallagher is far too busy to take time out from his chores for horse-riding lessons," Alice said to her daughter.

"I told her I'll teach her to ride, and that's exactly what I meant. Unless you have an objection to her learning to ride."

"Mommy, please. I got my fingers crossed," Rebecca flashed Alice an appealing smile.

"No, I don't mind." Alice's cheeks flushed a light pink, emphasizing the blue of her eyes. "I just don't want to impose."

"Trust me, I'll be the first to tell you when you're imposing," he replied.

"Somehow I'm sure you will," she returned, her tone as dry as his had been.

He shot her a look of surprise. The pink of her cheeks intensified as she took Rebecca's hand in hers. "Lunch will be ready in thirty minutes," she said, then turned and traipsed back to the house.

He watched her go, noting the subtle sway of her hips, the rigid set of her back. That was the second time she'd exhibited a spark of spirit that surprised him.

On the surface she looked meek, life-beaten, but it was obvious she wasn't down for the count. He eyed the mare in the corral and smiled as he thought of Rebecca wondering how he'd caught the horse in a box.

Monsters. What kind did a six-year-old dream about? Suddenly Cam found himself wanting to get at the heart of what bogeymen haunted Rebecca's sleep, frightening her enough that she wanted to learn how to ride a horse really fast. The very "people monsters" that she was afraid wanted to take her away from her mommy.

Cameron liked Rebecca. Kids were easy to like. They hadn't yet learned to be devious, to smoothly lie or take advantage of friendship. He'd almost forgotten that there were still human beings left that retained a core of goodness, a heart of innocence. Kids and animals. They were the only ones Cameron trusted…kids, animals and his sister, Elena.

With lunch only a half an hour away, he didn't want to begin working with the horse. Instead he turned and eyed the house, making mental notes of all the exterior work he wanted to get done before winter set in.

He'd bought the ranch for a song from an old couple who'd decided to retire to Florida. From the condition of the place, the old man had unofficially retired a long time before they'd actually moved.

Although structurally sound, the house begged for a coat of paint and most of the shutters hung askew, needing new hardware to make them functional.

He'd lived here nearly a year and had bought the

house with the anticipation of a trust fund his parents had left him. He now had the money to turn this ranch into the successful venture he'd once dreamed of owning. Unfortunately somewhere along the line he'd lost those dreams. They had smothered to death beneath the weight of his anger, and the sense of betrayal that never left his mind…his heart.

He waved a hand in greeting as he saw several of his men in a truck coming from one of the distant pastures. With a squeal of dusty brakes, the truck pulled up next to where he stood.

"We're heading into town for lunch. Want to come along?" The question came from Emmett Cantrell, a grizzled old man who should have retired years before but still had enough spunk and energy to work. He rode in the back of the pickup along with three other men. The four of them and the two in the cab comprised the total of Cameron's work force.

"No thanks…got lunch waiting for me inside," Cameron replied.

The men waved and Cameron watched as the pickup headed down the long winding driveway to the blacktop road that would take them into Mustang. He knew they would return within an hour and be back to work. They were good men, hard workers who were grateful to have an opportunity to work through the approaching winter.

When Cameron entered the kitchen, Rebecca and Alice were just finishing their lunch. Alice jumped up from her chair at his appearance and quickly began clearing their dishes from the table.

"I thought I told you yesterday, there's no reason for you to eat before me," he said as he hung his hat on the rack just inside the door. "It makes double work and isn't productive. We can eat our meals together."

"Okay," she agreed. "From now on we eat all meals together." She looked at Rebecca, who remained at the table. "Finish your sandwich, then go change into one of your dresses. After lunch we're going to get you enrolled in school."

Rebecca's petite features pulled into a frown. "I don't wanna go to school. I want to just stay here and be a cowgirl."

Cameron eased into the chair next to her. "I'll tell you what...you go to school and each day, if the weather is nice, when you get home I'll give you a horseback-riding lesson."

Rebecca's eyes widened with excitement. "For real?" She narrowed her eyes thoughtfully. "You wouldn't tell me a lie, would you?"

Cameron shook his head. "I never say things I don't mean. Besides, I'm a cowboy, and cowboys don't lie."

"That's right! Cowboys don't lie! Can we start today?" Rebecca asked eagerly.

Cameron started to put her off, to tell her tomorrow was soon enough, but as he looked at her, he noticed the shadows that had haunted her eyes were momentarily gone. Nothing but childish excitement, innocent joy shone from them now.

"Sure, we'll start today."

Rebecca shoved away from the table. "I'm done

eating, Mommy. I'll go put on my dress and we can go to school.'' She jumped up and down with ill-contained excitement, then flew from the kitchen and up the stairs.

''Thank you,'' Alice said softly as she set a plate before him. ''That was very kind of you. She hasn't had much to look forward to the last couple of months.''

Cameron nodded curtly, although he didn't particularly like the idea of Alice thinking he was kind. He wasn't. All his kindness had smothered beneath the weight of his bitterness. All his gentleness had disappeared on the day he'd walked into his bedroom and found Ginny and Samuel in bed together.

They both jumped as a knock sounded at the front door. Alice hurried from the kitchen to answer and Cameron followed just behind, stifling a groan as he saw the plump older woman peering through the door screen.

Millicent Creighton. Mustang's very own queen gossip. And she was wearing one of her crazy hats, which meant she was on duty, ready to pounce on any tidbit of gossip that could be used in her weekly social column.

''Yoohoo. Hello, Cameron.'' She tapped polished nails on the screen.

Alice stepped aside and Cameron opened the door. ''Hello, Millicent. What can I do for you?''

''I was just in town and saw some of your men at the café. Burt Winston told me you'd hired a housekeeper, somebody new to town. I thought I'd drop by and welcome her.''

"Alice Burwell, meet Millicent Creighton. Millicent writes a weekly social column for the *Mustang Monitor*," Cameron said.

Millicent took Alice's hand and bobbed her head, the movement causing her ridiculous hat to slip forward on her forehead. Her hat appeared to be a celebration of fall, bedecked with pinecones, acorns and red and yellow leaves.

Alice seemed transfixed by the hat as the two shook hands. "Burwell. Are you part of the Burwells from Billings?" Millicent asked as Cameron ushered them into the living room, where the two women sat on the sofa.

"Uh…no. No relation," Alice replied. She tore her gaze from Millicent's hat and offered a tentative smile. "We're from back east."

"We?" Millicent's gray brows danced upward, disappearing beneath the brim of the hat. "Are you married?"

"No…widowed. I have a daughter."

"Oh, how nice." Millicent reached into her large purse and pulled out a notepad. "I just thought I'd do a little paragraph about you in the paper this week, you know, an introduction to the town."

Cameron saw the flare of terror that suddenly filled Alice's eyes. It was there only a moment, then gone. "Oh, that's not necessary!" she exclaimed. "Besides, I'm not interesting enough to warrant a whole paragraph in the paper."

"But it's a wonderful way to get people to know you," Millicent pressed.

Alice shook her head. "Please, I'd rather not be in the paper."

"And you know I don't like people knowing my business," Cameron added. He was rewarded with a smile of gratitude from Alice.

Millicent sniffed and stuffed her notepad back in her purse. "I'm having a terrible time getting a column together this week. Things have been so boring around here."

"Go talk to Elena." Cameron walked back to the front door, a not so subtle indication that Millicent's business was finished here. "I'm sure that new nephew of mine has smiled or burped or done something she'll think warrants a mention in the paper."

Millicent stood and knocked her hat back in place with one pudgy hand. "It's a sad turn of events when I'm relegated to writing about baby gas." She walked to the door and turned back to Alice. "It was nice meeting you, dear. Let me know if you change your mind about a little mention in my column."

Alice nodded and Millicent left. Cameron closed the door and turned to face Alice. She averted her gaze from him. "I'll just finish up in the kitchen," she said.

He followed her and sat back down at the table. As he ate his sandwich, she cleaned up, her back to him as she scrubbed down the countertops.

"Exactly where back east are you from?" he asked.

She whirled around, eyes wide. "Uh…a small town outside of Pittsburgh, Pennsylvania."

She was lying. He could see the lie in the shifting of her eyes, hear it in the tension of her voice. But why? And why had she been so terrified that Millicent Creighton might mention her name in the paper?

He watched her for another long moment, wondering what she was afraid of…what secrets she harbored. Was she really a destitute widow or something else altogether?

He felt the same surge of energy he used to feel when he was on a case, hunting prey that would eventually yield him a paycheck. He welcomed the rush of adrenaline. He'd kept himself numb for so long, afraid of the pain that always waited in the wings to claim him. But this emotion…curiosity and intrigue, felt clean and good.

He no longer intended to fire Alice Burwell. He intended to ferret out her secrets, find out exactly what had brought her to Mustang and to his ranch.

She better hope that his instincts were wrong, that she hadn't lied to him about who she was and the situation that had brought her here. For there was nothing Cameron hated worse than lies.

His life in the last year had been filled with duplicity and deception. First Samuel and Ginny's deceit, then more of the same from the people who had attempted to steal his trust fund.

He'd had enough lies to last him a lifetime. Alice better hope she'd told him the truth, for if Cameron discovered she'd lied, she'd be out of the job and out of his house so fast her head would spin.

Chapter 4

"I figured it was about time I got myself over here to meet my brother's new housekeeper." The attractive, dark-haired woman on the porch smiled and held out a hand to Alicia. "Hi, I'm Elena Richards. Cameron mentioned last week that he'd hired somebody."

"I'm Alice Burwell. It's nice to meet you." Alicia shook Elena's warm hand and opened the door further to invite her in. She'd been working for Cameron for two weeks and other than Millicent Creighton's visit, there had been no other visitors.

Elena stopped short as she stepped into the living room and looked around in obvious astonishment. "Cameron said he'd hired a housekeeper, he didn't mention you were a miracle worker as well."

Alicia smiled with warm pleasure. She knew Elena was talking about the condition of the living room. Alicia's hard work over the last two weeks had paid off. The wood floors shone in the midafternoon light that streamed in through the spotless windows. Without the black soot that had covered them, the fireplace stones now gleamed with natural beauty and the oak furniture in the room glowed with a coating of lemon oil.

"There's still a lot to be done, but I think I've made good headway," Alicia said.

Elena laughed. "Good headway? Trust me, whatever Cameron is paying you, it isn't half enough."

Alicia returned her smile. "I'm quite happy with what he's paying me." It was true. Her first two week's pay now rested in an envelope in her dresser drawer. Although far from being enough for a legal defense fund, it was a start. "How about a cup of coffee?"

"Hmm, sounds wonderful," Elena agreed and followed Alicia into the kitchen.

"I would have come by to say hello sooner but my son has been sick. He's had an ear infection that has kept him fussy. My husband, Trent, decided to give me a little break today so he's home babysitting." Elena nodded her thanks as Alicia set a steaming cup of coffee before her.

"How old is your boy?" Alicia asked as she poured herself a cup of coffee and joined the attractive woman at the table.

"Five months, although everyone still talks about him as if he's a newborn. There hasn't been another baby born in Mustang since mine." Elena's face took on the glow of new motherhood. "And naturally I think he's the cutest, brightest baby ever born.''

''Naturally,'' Alicia agreed with a laugh. She liked Elena, whose dark eyes radiated a natural warmth and friendliness. It was difficult to believe she was sister to the man who hadn't cracked a smile or breathed a word of friendliness in the two weeks Alicia had been working for him.

''You have a child, don't you? I think Cameron mentioned a daughter?''

Alicia nodded. ''Rebecca. She's six years old.''

''Ah, first-grader? Has she settled into school out here?''

''Yes, we got her started the second day we were here. Thankfully she loves school, but I'm not sure if it's school itself she loves or what happens directly after school. Cameron has been teaching her to ride a horse.''

Elena stared at her in disbelief. ''My brother, Mr. Dour Personality?''

Alicia stifled a laugh at Elena's snap characterization. ''Actually, he's quite good with Rebecca. He only growls and grunts at me.''

Elena continued to eye Alicia with a touch of speculation. ''Don't let him run you off. He's been alone for too long. I know he can be quite difficult, but he needs somebody to pull him out of his self-imposed cocoon of isolation.''

An embarrassed little laugh escaped from Alicia. ''I'm just his housekeeper. Nothing more.'' She felt the warmth of a blush on her cheeks.

Yes, she was just a housekeeper, but she was a

housekeeper developing an overwhelming attraction and preoccupation with her boss. She felt her blush intensify as Elena's gaze remained locked on her, as intense and probing as her brother's.

Elena smiled again, as if whatever she'd seen deep within Alicia she liked. She sipped her coffee, then set the cup back in the saucer. "It will be nice having another woman so close when winter comes."

"I've heard the winters out here can be pretty rough," Alicia said.

Elena nodded. "Brutal. Last winter was unusually mild, but all the forecasters are calling for a doozy this year. You have to be of sturdy stock to endure the isolation of a Montana blizzard."

"Trust me, I'm strong enough to endure." Alicia thought back over the past year of her life. She'd endured more than she'd ever believed herself capable of…a blizzard or two was nothing.

"You'll have to bring your little girl over for a visit. I've got a little poodle who would love to play with her."

"Oh, Rebecca would love that. She adores animals," Alicia exclaimed.

"And my little Spooky loves everyone." Elena took another sip of her coffee, then stood. "I'd better get back home. My handsome husband is strong and courageous until little Travis cries, then Trent falls apart."

Alicia smiled with understanding. Robert had been the same…utterly helpless in the face of his daughter's tears. As Elena stood, Alicia did the same and walked with her to the front door.

"Thank you for stopping by. The only other person I've met is Millicent Creighton," Alicia said. "And I'm afraid I didn't make her very happy."

Elena laughed. "Millicent isn't happy unless you're whispering deep dark secrets in her ear that she can then tell to the world in her column."

"She wanted to do a little introduction of me in the paper and I asked her not to."

Elena nodded with apparent understanding. "If you were raised like me, you were taught that you get your name in the paper three times in your life...when you're born, get married and get buried. Any more than that is considered scandalous." She took Alicia's hand and squeezed it. "Anyway, I'm glad you're here and I hope we'll be good friends."

"Me, too." Alicia watched as Elena turned and lightly ran down the porch steps toward her car. When she reached the vehicle she turned and waved.

When Elena's car disappeared from sight, she turned and went back into the kitchen. As she cleared their cups from the table, she thought of Elena's parting words.

Yes, it would be nice to have a friend...but how close could she get to any friend without jeopardizing their safety? How many lies would she have to tell, how many times would she have to bite her tongue, pretend that everything was fine and her life was normal?

Oh, it would be so wonderful to have a friend to talk to, to confide in. It would be so good to talk to somebody about Robert's death, to divulge her fears about Robert's parents' attempt to gain custody of Rebecca, and Alicia's subsequent running away to keep her daughter safe with her.

Unfortunately, she'd had to face some hard truths about her relationship with Robert, and she knew Broderick would have offered a small fortune for any information regarding her whereabouts. Even if she decided to trust a few of the new people in her life, there was always a chance they might whisper something to somebody else and her daughter would be forfeited for a quick, healthy reward.

Broderick and Ruth Randall had destroyed their son—her husband—with their unnatural coldness, their wicked manipulations and their impossible standards. And Alicia would never...ever allow them the opportunity to do the same to Rebecca.

No, it was better to have acquaintances than good friends, better to have surface relationships with everyone until the threat of Broderick and Ruth no longer existed. She shivered slightly, wondering if that day would ever come.

Looking at her watch, she realized her daughter would be home from school in an hour. Enrolling Rebecca in the Mustang Elementary School had been one of the first tests of establishing their new identities.

The school secretary had requested Rebecca's birth certificate and a copy of her immunization records. Alicia had covered the immunization problem by mumbling something about religious reasons then had promised to send for the paperwork and hoped in the meantime the school would forget all about them. She couldn't provide a birth certificate because she knew that enrolling Rebecca under her real name would leave a paper trail that could be followed.

As she pulled a roast out of the refrigerator and put it in a pot on the stove to cook for dinner, she thought of her conversation with Elena.

Mr. Dour Personality…that's what Elena had called her brother. In the two weeks Alicia had been working for him, she had found Cameron Gallagher to be many things. Forbidding, aloof and uncompromising…he was all those.

However, there were times when she felt his gaze lingering on her…a gaze filled with curiosity and something else…something far more evocative, far more dangerous. Even now, just thinking about that expression in his eyes, a wave of heat swept through her.

She wondered what it would be like to be kissed by Cameron. His mouth had a natural sexuality…a full lower lip and a strong upper. She had a feeling kissing Cameron would be like relinquishing your soul. His intensity would make it impossible not to respond, impossible to hang on to any vestige of self.

As she made his bed each morning, she found herself running a hand over his body-warmed sheets, wondering how it would feel to be held in his arms, pulled against his firm chest.

She assumed most of these disturbing thoughts were because she was alone…so achingly alone, and lonely, and in the past several months had come to realize that what she'd felt for Robert had been less love and more gratitude.

Robert's lovemaking hadn't come close to touching the well of passion Alicia knew she possessed deep inside. She longed for a man to make her feel the kind of desire she'd only read about in books…the heart-halting, breath-stealing kind of passion that she'd seen in movies, but had never experienced herself.

As she added water to the browning roast, she chided herself for her fanciful thoughts. The kind of passion she longed for was probably an invention of Hollywood that had nothing to do with real people and real life.

She shook her head and began peeling potatoes, inwardly laughing at her own foolishness. She was a woman on the run, a woman who'd sacrificed everything for the safety of her daughter. Desire, passion and love-ever-after hardly had a place in her life at the moment.

''Cameron, watch out!''

Burt's warning came a second too late for Cameron to dodge the roll of barbed wire fencing that fell off the back of the truck. The roll caught him in the upper back and slid down his buttocks then bounced to the ground, but not before it had taken his shirt and a layer of skin with it.

''Boss! Are you all right?'' Burt hurried over to Cameron.

Cameron let loose a string of oaths as he plucked

at his shirt, felt the burn of deeply lacerated flesh. Burt stepped behind him and clucked his tongue like an old woman. "Gosh, Boss, we'd better go get you cleaned up. You've got some pretty good gouges there."

"Yeah. I'll take Bandit and head back to the house." Cameron released another round of swearing as he reached a hand around his back and felt the slashed condition of his shirt.

"Are you sure you don't want me to get you home?"

"No, I'll be okay. I need you to stay here and finish up. See if you and the men can get the last of that old fencing out and get some of the new fence in place."

Moments later, on the back of Bandit, a huge black steed, Cameron headed for the house. As he rode, he cursed again, angry with himself for not paying close enough attention. He and his men had begun work at dawn, removing all the old barbed wire in the west pasture in anticipation of putting up new.

Nothing irritated Cameron more than carelessness, and he'd been careless to turn his back on a teetering pile of barbed wire rolls. And what irritated him more than anything was that he knew his unusual carelessness was provoked by a preoccupation with his housekeeper. He'd been thinking of her instead of keeping his mind on his work.

He nudged Bandit into an all-out run, enjoying the speed, the chilly wind in his face, the adrenaline that pumped through him as the horse tore across brown pasture.

As he rode, his thoughts whirled. His house had never been in such good order. Each morning he awakened to fresh coffee and a hearty breakfast, and in the evenings he walked into a spotless house with a warm meal waiting for him.

More than these mundane creature comforts, he found Alice Burwell an easy woman to be around. Unlike most women he knew, who prattled mindlessly to fill any moment of awkward silence, Alice seemingly felt no need to hear her own voice fill up a void.

Nor had she tried to change any of his bad habits. She didn't nag him about wiping his feet when he came in, didn't censure him when he forgot to put away his shaving cream or throw his towel in the hamper. And it was these very unimposing traits about her that had made him reluctant to dig too deeply into her story. He didn't want to discover if she'd lied, because then he'd have to do something about it.

He slowed Bandit as he reached the stables. Dismounting, he put the horse in one of the stalls, then headed toward the house, his back still burning as if on fire.

He entered the house through the backdoor. As he stepped into the kitchen the scent of a simmering roast greeted him. Although it was not quite four o'clock, the table was already set for dinner.

There was a sense of welcoming in the sight. He felt as if he'd stepped into somebody else's house…a house where a family sat at the table and shared the events of the day. This thought darkened his mood. He wanted no family, no ties to bind his heart.

He strode out of the kitchen and met Alice on the stairs.

"Oh, you're home earlier than usual today," she said. She stood on the top stair, her blue eyes retaining a hint of surprise.

He frowned and advanced up. "I had a little accident."

She stepped aside as he reached the top. As he walked past her she gasped. "Oh, Cameron…your back!"

"Yeah, I managed to tangle with a roll of barbed wire," he explained. "I'm sure it will be fine. I'll just jump in the shower and wash off."

"You need more than a shower. Those wounds need to be washed out with antiseptic." She followed him into his bedroom.

He ignored her, wincing as he peeled off the shirt. It was torn to shreds and encrusted with blood. He wadded it up into a ball and tossed it into the wastebasket. "I'll be fine," he said to Alice as he waved a hand to dismiss her. "I'll take care of it."

She gazed at him in disbelief. "Unless you are a contortionist, I don't see how you intend to manage it." With hands on her hips, she eyed him narrowly. "You said you tangled with barbed wire? Do you need a tetanus shot? I won't have you getting lockjaw because you didn't get cleaned up properly."

He sank down on the edge of the bed, realizing

she was right. "No, I had a tetanus shot last year. There's a first-aid kit under the sink in the bathroom. It should have whatever you might need in it."

She disappeared and returned several moments later with the first-aid kit in hand and a basin of warm water and several hand towels.

He leaned forward as she began to dab at the wounds with a warm, wet cloth. The warm water soothed the burning sensation and he closed his eyes with a sigh of relief. As the sting dissipated, he began to notice other things.

He could smell her...a subtle floral scent mingling with a touch of musk. It was a scent that had attracted and disturbed him every day for the past two weeks.

"I'm going to use some hydrogen peroxide on these cuts," she murmured, her breath a whisper of warmth on his neck. "It's going to sting quite a bit."

He nodded.

"I met your sister today. She stopped by to say hello. She's very nice."

"Yeah." He stiffened as she dabbed his back with the cold peroxide.

"Have you two always been close?" Again the whisper of her breath warmed Cameron's neck, beckoning a shiver he fought against.

He tried to focus on her words, not on the sensations her nearness evoked. "Elena and I have always been friends as well as siblings," he replied.

"It must have been nice...growing up together."

There was a wistfulness in her tone that reached

deep inside him and plucked the memory of happy times in childhood, when he'd been in the bosom of his loving family...before the taste of adulthood and the bitterness of betrayal.

Looking in the mirror of the dresser, he could see her reflection. Her lower lip was captured between her teeth and a frown creased her forehead as she gently applied the antiseptic. She winced each time she touched his back, as if she felt the stinging herself.

"You don't have brothers or sisters?" he asked.

"No. My parents were intelligent. They only had *one* mistake." She compressed her lips together, as if irritated with herself for saying too much.

Her fingertips were soft...comforting and Cameron felt himself responding to her gentle touch. Transfixed by her reflection, he continued to watch her.

When had she lost the purple shadows beneath her eyes? No longer did she have those dark bruises, rather her skin glowed with health and the drawn appearance she'd had when she'd first arrived had disappeared. Even her hair appeared softer...slightly lighter in color and curled to frame her face.

Her gaze captured his in the mirror and suddenly the air around them seemed thicker, making it difficult for him to catch a breath.

They froze...two images in the mirror. Her hands remained on his back, warm imprints that stirred something deep inside him. Her sapphire eyes widened and her lips parted, whether in surprise or in invitation, he wasn't sure.

All he knew for certain was that he wanted her. He wanted her now, this moment. He wanted her in his bed, naked and eager beneath him. It was a wanting that had been building from the moment he'd opened his door and saw her standing on his front porch.

He averted his gaze from the mirror and stood. Her hands fell away from his back as he turned to look at her. "Thank you," he said, his voice husky and deep.

"You're welcome." Her reply was breathless.

He took a single step toward her.

She didn't retreat.

His heart pounded in his chest as he stepped closer yet…so close he could feel the heat of her body radiating outward.

In the depths of her eyes, he saw desire. Glimmering, shining, it reached out to him, silently offering surrender. He had a feeling all he had to do was reach out and touch her…stroke her lips with the pad of his thumb, caress her cheek with his forefinger and she would succumb instantly.

In the distance, a horn honked, a familiar sound at this time of day. The sound broke whatever energy radiated between them.

"That's the school bus. I need to go meet Rebecca." Still, Alice remained motionless, as if trapped in place by invisible strands.

Cameron knew the bus dropped Rebecca at the end of the long, winding driveway and the driver always honked so Alice would know to meet her daughter. "You'd better go."

Suddenly Cameron was the one who wanted out…needed to be away from her, distanced from her sweet fragrance, separated from the winsome look in her eyes.

"I'm going out," he said abruptly as he grabbed a shirt from the closet. "The best medicine for me at the moment is a couple of beers at the Roundup. Don't hold dinner for me." He didn't wait for a reply.

He buttoned his shirt as he took the stairs two at a time to the front door. Instead of taking his truck, he headed for the stables and Bandit. Within moments he was back on the horse.

As he rode down the driveway he passed Alice and Rebecca coming from the bus stop. He felt a moment of contrition as he realized Rebecca would be disappointed to miss her daily riding lesson. With a determined sigh, he shoved the guilt aside.

She wasn't his kid, wasn't his responsibility. He didn't owe her anything and it was just as well she learn early about disappointments and heartache.

He gave Bandit his head, allowing him the freedom to race toward the tavern on the edge of town. He knew what he was doing…trying to outrun his desire, hoping to leave it someplace behind him on the narrow two-lane road.

It had been two years…two years since Ginny had disappeared and Sam had been arrested…two years in which Cameron had survived by keeping himself numb. Somehow…someway, something about Alice Burwell had managed to sneak through his veil of numbness.

It took him over an hour to get to town. He hadn't pushed Bandit hard, but had kept him at a steady gait. Cameron reined in as he approached the Roundup, a one-story wooden structure with a neon cowboy flashing from the flat roof. As usual, pickup trucks and 4x4 vehicles filled the parking lot, and raucous music poured out of the door as it opened and closed with the comings and goings of patrons.

He dismounted and tied Bandit to the hitching post that was rarely used except in the summer and then only by the staunchest of horsemen.

It had been months since Cameron had ventured into the Roundup. Never particularly social, in the past two years he'd become a loner and had never been really comfortable in the smoky, crowded tavern.

He found a table in the corner, as far away from the guitar-twanging jukebox as possible. As he sat, he raised a hand in acknowledgement to several of the men who stood at the bar.

"Well, well, look what the cat dragged in." Amanda Creighton greeted him, her eyes sparkling flirtatiously as she pulled an order pad from her pocket. "I thought maybe you'd moved out of town or something. It's been so long since you've been in."

He smiled at her. He'd always enjoyed Amanda's company. He had a feeling Amanda didn't quite know where she fit, both in the town of Mustang and in life in general. "I'd never move without coming by to give you a goodbye kiss," he replied.

She laughed. "Ah, you're a talker, Cameron Gallagher. What can I get you? The usual?"

He nodded and watched as she walked away. Amanda was attractive, and he thought they might be kindred spirits, two souls with battle-scarred hearts seeking solace. The difference was Cameron sought peace in keeping himself separate from others and he suspected Amanda hid a heartache behind her too-bright smile and bad-girl aura.

Yes, Amanda was attractive, although any man seeking a relationship with her would have to put up with Amanda's mother, Millicent. Still, Millicent Creighton didn't bother Cameron. Unfortunately there were no sparks of any kind between him and Amanda. They were friendly with each other, flirtatious and teasing…and not interested in anything more.

Cameron wasn't interested at all in pursuing any woman. Dead men didn't need love, and Cameron had considered himself a dead man for a long time. He had no illusions about his future…if he had one at all, it would be lived alone.

As he continued to watch Amanda, her features seemed to fade as a vision of Alice superimposed itself into his head. Those vivid blue eyes…the mouth that looked as if it needed to be kissed hard and long…damn. Although he had no desire for a relationship with the woman, he definitely had a desire for something with his housekeeper.

It had been a long time since he'd wanted anything from a woman…a long time since the pit of his stomach had ached with physical want. Something about Alice had awakened him, stirred the desire that had been stifled inside him, and he didn't like it. He didn't like it one little bit. He preferred his cocoon of safe numbness, and desperately wanted it back.

Amanda returned with a frosty mug of beer. As she plunked it down before him, he wondered how many he'd have to drink before he'd stop wanting Alice Burwell.

Chapter 5

"Mommy? Can we stay here forever?" Rebecca peeked at Alicia from beneath the blankets on her bed. "I really like it here."

Alicia leaned down and kissed her daughter's forehead, then sat on the edge of her bed. "You know this is just the place I'm working for now. This is Mr. Gallagher's house, but someday we'll have our own house, someplace special just for the two of us."

Rebecca's forehead furrowed with a frown. "But I think here is special and we should just stay. Mr. Lallagher doesn't mind us being here. It's a really big house with lots of room."

Alicia rubbed her thumb across the little girl's wrinkled forehead. "I think it's time for you to close your eyes and go to sleep and stop worrying about all this. We're here now and I'm glad you like it here.'' She gave Rebecca one final kiss, then turned off the light and left the room.

In her own room, she changed into her night-gown, pulled on her robe, then went back downstairs, too restless for sleep. She sank onto the sofa and leaned her head back, trying to relax.

Rebecca was happy here...happier than Alicia had seen her in months. She loved school, adored Sugar, the horse Cameron was teaching her to ride, and was beginning to look at Cameron just as she had once gazed at her father.

"Damn you, Robert," she sighed tiredly. "Damn you for dying and leaving me to fight your family all alone." Tears pressed ominously, burning behind her eyes.

She drew in several deep breaths, knowing it wasn't grief for Robert that caused the threat of tears, but rather the knowledge that even if Robert had lived, she'd probably be in the same set of circumstances.

She realized now that she and Robert would have never stayed together, that the gratitude she'd felt for him, the gentle friendship they'd shared, hadn't been vital enough, essential enough to keep them together forever. Eventually she would have wanted more and she would have left him, opening the door for Broderick and Ruth to fight her for custody of Rebecca.

Pressing her fingers against her temples, she realized what bothered her more than anything...Cameron. In the space of two short weeks he had managed to summon in her the kind of passion, the sort of wild desire that had been lacking in her relationship with Robert. It both terrified her and thrilled her at the same time.

Still, she knew she'd be a fool to allow anything to happen between herself and Cameron. He was her boss and she desperately needed this job. Adding in any kind of personal relationship to the employer/employee mix would be the height of foolishness.

However, what frightened her was that there was a part of her that longed to be foolish, that wanted to hide in heady passion, lose herself even momentarily in the mindlessness of complete desire. It would be wonderful for just a single moment to forget the fear that had driven her for the last couple of months and simply feel like a normal woman.

Her fingers tingled as she remembered the feel of Cameron's skin beneath them. His back was tanned, warm as if it had retained the kiss of the sun and she'd fought the impulse to caress instead of take care of his wounds.

"Time for bed," she said aloud, not wanting to dwell on the naked emotion she'd seen in his eyes as they had faced each other, an emotion that had sent him running out of the house for the night.

She'd recognized it, pure and unadulterated lust. Apparently he, too, realized the foolishness of following through on it.

"Go to bed, Alicia," she instructed herself aloud, irritated by her crazy thoughts. She couldn't jeopardize her position here by allowing things between them to flare out of control. Rebecca was happy here and at least for a while they had no place else to go. That, was the bottom line.

She stood and moved to the front door, unsure whether to lock it or leave it unlocked for Cameron's return. As she contemplated her choices, she heard the sound of hooves approaching.

Knowing the smart thing to do was scamper up the stairs and into her bedroom, her body ignored her brain and instead she opened the door just in time to see Cameron riding down the long drive toward the house.

As he reached the area just outside the front door, the horse reared up on hind legs and whinnied. In the bright illumination of the moonlight, Cameron's gaze met hers...his eyes glittering silver in the lunar light. In an instant the horse was back on all fours and headed for the stables.

Alicia's breath remained caught in her throat and remained there even when the horse and rider disappeared from her view. In that single instant, with the horse pawing the air and Cameron sitting tall and proud, he had never looked more like the quintessential cowboy.

There had been a wildness in his eyes...as if he were one with the powerful animal beneath him and the cold wind that sung in the air.

Again her brain commanded she go up to her room, make herself scarce rather than face Cameron. But she felt as if there was a short circuit between brain and body, between good sense and foolishness. And then it was too late. He appeared on the porch before her.

He tipped his hat, a mocking smile curving the corners of his lips. "Good evening. How kind of you to wait up for me."

"I didn't. I was on my way to bed when I heard the sound of one of your horses." Alicia backed up as he stepped into the house, far too close to her. He smelled of the night air and of leather, soap and beer, a combination inherently male, and overwhelmingly attractive.

He closed the door behind him, then turned to look at her again. The wildness in his eyes softened and his hand reached out and touched her hair. "What color is it naturally?" He didn't wait for her answer as his fingers curled around a strand. "I'll bet it's the color of corn silk."

"I...yes, it's light blond." The words came with difficulty as her breath was caught inside her chest.

"Why did you color it?"

He stood so close to her she could see that his eyes weren't really black, as she'd initially thought, but rather a dark brown flecked with black. She tried to focus on his question and not on his heart-stopping nearness. "I just wanted to try something new."

He released the strand of hair and instead stroked a finger down the side of her face. "Tell me, Alice Burwell, what should we do about this energy...this chemistry...that exists between us?" His voice was low, husky and she realized she would look a fool if she pretended she didn't know what he was talking about.

"I don't know," she replied, wishing he would

step away…stand closer…leave her alone…kiss her.

He rubbed a finger across her lower lip, his touch scalding her mouth with heat that infused her entire body. She fought the impulse to open her mouth, draw his finger inside and taste him.

His eyes flared, as if he sensed the impulse she fought against. His hand dropped and he took a step backward. "Go to bed, Alice." He raked a hand through his wind-tossed hair. "I've had too much to drink."

She hesitated, knowing she should leave… run…yet not wanting to. "Should I make some coffee?"

"It's not coffee I want, or need." Still his gaze blazed, speaking more than words, speaking the language of desire.

Alicia wanted to fall into that fire, be consumed by the flames and she took a step toward him. She heard him breathe inward, as if shocked by her nearness. In a single, swift movement, he reached out and grabbed her, then pulled her intimately against him.

Her eyes widened as her body melded to his, felt the power of his shoulders beneath her hands, felt the thrust of his hips and the evidence of his desire. A moan escaped her, a deep throaty moan she couldn't control.

His hands moved down her back and cupped her buttocks, pressed her closer, more deeply into him. At the same time his lips touched the side of her neck, the sensitive point just below her ear. His lips scalded her, branding her with heat and she allowed her head to fall back, giving him access to the column of her throat at the same time his hips moved suggestively against hers.

This is crazy, a little voice whispered inside her head, but she didn't want to listen. She didn't want sanity at the moment; she wanted Cameron. She smoothed her hands across his shoulders, fingers clutching and her breath quickened as his hands moved from her buttocks, up her sides, where he lightly touched the swell of each breast.

Alicia was on fire, each and every nerve ending screaming for attention, for his touch. Her silk robe had initially been cool against her skin, but now it was too hot, demanded to be shrugged off, exposing more skin to his fingers, his lips.

He seemed to know her desire, and with a quick flip of the belt, he tugged the robe off her shoulders, allowing it to fall into a pool at their feet.

This time when he touched her breasts through the thin material of her gown, it felt as if she were naked to his touch. Her nipples grew taut, as if trying to burst free from the confines of the wispy nightgown.

Control…she could feel it slipping away. She wanted him to take her, didn't want to think of consequences at the moment. "Cameron." She whispered his name against his shoulder. He stiffened, as if her voice brought him back from some precarious brink.

He raised his head and looked at her, his eyes dark and hungry. "You want me to take you right here? On the floor?'' His voice was deeper than usual, almost harsh in tone.

Alicia blinked, felt the mood shifting. "I don't...I want..." She stumbled over the words as her brain refused to function.

He dropped his hands from her, leaned down and picked up her robe. "Go to bed, Alice," he demanded.

"But..." She wasn't sure what she intended to say.

"Go to your room," he thundered.

She ran up the stairs like the hounds of hell nipped at her heels. But, it wasn't the hounds of hell she feared, it was the devil in blue jeans, the devil named Cameron.

In her room, she shrugged out of her robe and climbed into bed, her eyes focused on the door. He wanted her. She'd seen it in his eyes, felt it in his touch. He wanted her and God help her, she wanted him.

Would he come to her? Would he sneak into her room, make his way through the shaft of moonlight that filtered through her window?

She trembled at the thought, the quiver of her body not a result of fear, but the result of something much more intense. She remained watching the door for a very long time. When she finally fell asleep, she wasn't sure if she felt regret, or relief that he hadn't entered her room.

Cameron opened one eye and squinted against the faint morning light. Eight beers and the only thing he had managed to do was give himself one hell of a hangover.

There had been a time when he'd been able to knock back twice as many beers, but that had been right after Ginny's disappearance and Samuel's arrest, when Cameron had plunged into a downward spiral of self-destruction. But his flirtation with booze had lasted only a couple of weeks, then his keen sense of survival had kicked in and he'd moved to Mustang to start over.

He eased himself to a sitting position, gasping as his head threatened to split in half and fall apart. Damn. He'd been a fool to try to drown his attraction to Alice in the bottom of a bottle of beer.

It hadn't worked. The moment he'd stood in front of her last night, the anesthetizing effect of the beer had instantly dissipated. His hand itched as he remembered the feel of her silken hair beneath his fingertips. Her skin had been soft…so soft and enticingly warm.

With a sigh of irritation, he rolled out of bed. Ignoring the pounding of his head, he pulled on a pair of jeans and headed for the bathroom. What he needed was a pulsing hot shower to take away the headache, and an invigorating cold shower to ease the heat of his thoughts.

In the bathroom, he twisted around to get a vision of his back in the mirror. The wounds were easily visible, starting to scab over, but there was no telltale radiating redness to warn of infection.

Twenty minutes later he dressed for the day, realizing he'd slept later than he could remember. His unusual late morning was not only due to the fact that he'd drank too much, but also because the day was overcast and gray. He guessed it to be after nine o'clock as he left his bedroom.

He heard Alice in the kitchen as he walked down the stairs. She was humming a melody along with the radio. He paused on the bottom step. The sweet female sound mingling with the strains of music once again stirred the desire he'd hoped had gurgled down the shower drain.

Why, oh why was fate making things difficult on him? Why couldn't he feel this same kind of physical craving for Amanda…or any of the other eligible women the town of Mustang had to offer? Why did it have to be his housekeeper who magically stirred him?

"Good morning." She greeted him without looking at him as he walked into the kitchen. "Coffee?"

"Yeah…about a gallon." He sank into a chair at the table and watched as she poured him a cup. Clad in a pale pink sweater and a pair of designer jeans that hugged the shapely length of her legs, she looked far too attractive for his present mood.

"You've got nice clothes for a woman who was living in her car before this job," he observed. Maybe if he focused on the inconsistencies of her story, his initial gut feeling that she had lied to him, then his desire for her would quickly ebb.

She smoothed a hand down her sweater. "My husband was very generous during our marriage."

Cameron took a sip of his coffee and continued looking at her thoughtfully. "A man who was generous while alive, yet made no provisions for his wife and daughter in the event of his death?''

She shrugged, again her gaze averted from his. ''I guess it was the arrogance of youth. Robert was young, the last thing on his mind was death.''

''How did he die?''

''A car accident.'' She frowned, her brow furrowing.

''He was coming home from a late evening meeting with his fa…uh…boss and took a corner too fast. His car crashed into a tree. Robert was badly hurt. He held on for two days, then passed away.''

Cameron's gut told him she wasn't lying. Her voice held a well of sadness that couldn't be manufactured with lies. He sipped his coffee and considered her loss. How devastating it must be to lose a wife or a husband…somebody you had built a life with for years, someone you intended to grow old with.

He and Ginny's life together had barely begun. They'd lived together for three months before he'd walked in on her and Samuel that fateful day. Alice had to be one strong woman to deal with her grief and continue to face life head-on. He could almost admire strength of that kind. But of course, Alice had a child. Rebecca was her reason to go on. When Ginny had left, Cameron had been left with nothing but unfulfilled dreams and the taste of bitter betrayal lingering in his mouth.

''You told me to tell you when I needed groceries. I've got a list of things,'' she said, as if relieved to change the subject.

"I'll take you into town this morning and we can pick up what you need. I've got a few things I have to order from the feed store." Cameron drained his coffee cup and stood. "Let me know when you're ready and we'll leave."

"Oh, just give me a minute or two and I'll be ready." She washed her hands and dried them, then hurried up the stairs toward her room.

Cameron walked to the backdoor and peered out to the corral, where the wild horse walked restlessly within the wooden confines. Despite his work with the animal over the past two weeks, the horse refused to trust him. She clung to her independence, her very wildness, as if it were a mantra of protection.

Eventually he would win her over. It was inevitable. And he had a feeling the only way to get Alice Burwell out from under his skin was to make love to her. He was beginning to believe that was inevitable as well.

"Okay, I'm ready."

Her voice pulled him from his thoughts and he turned from the window. He frowned as he noticed she'd applied lipstick and brushed her hair. The red lip color emphasized the sensuality of her lips and there was nothing more he wanted to do than nibble it off. "Then let's go," he said, his voice more growl than anything.

Moments later they were in Cameron's truck, headed for Mustang. Before leaving the house he'd pulled on a suede jacket against the chill of the day, and Alice had put on a chic jean jacket. Despite their warm dress, he turned on the heater, hoping the warm blowing air would dispel the bewitching scent of her that filled the small cab.

They rode in silence for a few minutes. Cameron shifted positions, wondering when it had happened that silence had become uncomfortable.

As he drove, he cast her surreptitious glances, noting how the denim jacket intensified the hue of her eyes, and the pink sweater beneath pulled color into her cheeks.

Upon their first meeting, the blue of her eyes had reminded him of Ginny, but he'd never felt this intense craving to make love to Ginny, his thoughts had never been muddled by desire where Ginny was concerned.

"You mentioned something when I first hired you about being estranged from your family." He grasped for conversation, needing to fill the silence, wanting to still his own thoughts.

She sighed and nodded. "My mother is an English professor and my father is a history professor. They like books and research and academia. Children have no place in their world. Children are messy and loud, demanding and needy. I was an accident and I learned very early on that I was on my own."

"Sounds tough," he observed.

She shrugged. "It wasn't easy or tough, it was just life as I knew it."

"So, how did you meet your husband?"

She smiled, a full smile that softened her features and filled her face with a warmth Cameron felt in the pit of his stomach. "I was working as a waitress in a truck stop and Robert stopped in for a piece of pie." Her smile faded slightly and her eyes took on the distant haze of memories.

"Your parents are professors, yet you were working in a truck stop?"

"I moved out of my parents home and into my own place when I graduated from high school. Their house didn't feel like my home, I needed to create my own space, so I took the job at the truck stop."

"And you met Robert there."

She nodded. "Robert wasn't real handsome, but he had a sweet smile and a caring nature. We dated a couple of months, and he swept me off my feet." Her cheeks took on a heightened hue of color. "I got pregnant and we married soon after. I was so young...and it felt so nice to have somebody who cared about me after all those years of growing up with my parents. I was a good wife to him. I was always supportive, encouraged him in everything he did."

"You don't have to justify anything to me," he replied, surprised by her vehemence in voicing her attributes as a wife.

She flushed again and laughed, an uneasy laugh. "I guess I'm trying to justify it to myself."

He eyed her curiously. "What do you mean?"

Again she stared out the window and frowned thoughtfully. "I didn't know it when I first met him, but Robert was quite wealthy. A lot of his, uh, friends thought I was nothing but a gold digger.

They believed I got pregnant on purpose, to trap Robert into marrying me.''

"Did you?"

His question caused her eyes to widen. "No!" The single word exploded from her, as if it were an answer she'd had to give a hundred times before.

She drew a deep breath, as if to steady her emotions. "No, I didn't get pregnant on purpose. But in the months since Robert's death, I've had to face the realization that part of his charm was the life he offered to me." She looked down at her hands clasped in her lap. "And if that makes me a gold digger, then maybe I was."

"A gold digger usually isn't somebody who winds up working as a housekeeper on a ranch in Montana," Cameron said, oddly touched by her obvious guilt.

She flashed him a grateful smile and again a coil of heat unfurled in the pit of Cameron's stomach. He pulled into a parking space in front of the grocery store, sorry he'd delved at all into her personal life. Each snippet of information he discovered about her only seemed to heighten his desire for her.

They got out of the truck and moved to the sidewalk. "I'm going to head on down to the feed store," Cameron said. "Buy what we need and just tell them to put it on my account." He sensed her sudden tension as her gaze shot over his shoulder. He turned to see Sheriff Jesse Wilder approaching them.

As usual, Jesse's stern features were set in a scowl. It seemed to Cameron that Jesse had been frowning ever since Elena had gotten married. Cameron liked Jesse, knew the man had once thought himself in love with Cameron's sister. But, what struck him now was the anxiety that seemed to be radiating from Alice as the sheriff advanced.

"Jesse," Cameron greeted the man.

"Morning," Jesse returned, his features relaxing into a smile as he looked at Alice. "I heard through the grapevine that Mustang had a couple of new residents. Sorry I haven't gotten out your way to properly introduce myself." He held out a hand toward Alice. "Sheriff Jesse Wilder, at your service."

"Alice. Alice Burwell. It's nice to meet you," Alice replied, looking as skittish as a rabbit caught in the crosshairs of a rifle. "Uh, if you gentlemen will excuse me, I'd better attend to the shopping." She whirled around and disappeared through the grocery store doors.

Jesse turned to Cameron with a grin. "Whew, she's quite a looker," he said.

"And she's quite taken." The words fell from his lips without volition.

Jesse's eyes widened in surprise. "You sly dog, you. No wonder you've kept her isolated out at your place. Hell, it's about time you showed a little interest in something other than those horses of yours."

"When are you gonna find a little woman and settle down?" Cameron returned.

Jesse sighed and raked a hand through his dark hair. "I don't know. Mustang seems to be lacking the kind of woman I'm looking for.'' He smiled wistfully. ''The good one got away from me.''

''She's happy, Jesse. Happier than I've ever seen her,'' Cameron said of his sister.

Jesse nodded, his features once again forming a frown. ''I know, and I'm glad for her. I hope someday to find the same happiness for myself.''

Cameron smiled darkly. ''I quit looking for happiness a long time ago.'' He clapped Jesse on the back. ''I've got to get down to the feed store. I'll see you later.''

As the two men parted ways, Cameron's mind spun with questions. There were so many inconsistencies in Alice's story.

She'd married a wealthy man, a man she said had no family, and yet upon his death she was left destitute? It didn't make sense. What had happened to her husband's wealth?

Something else that didn't make sense was why she had looked so damned frightened when she'd first seen Jesse coming toward them? Did she have a problem with law enforcement figures? Or was it possible the secrets he sensed she guarded were far more serious than he'd initially thought?

Most confusing of all was his own snap reply to Jesse. What in the hell had possessed him to tell Jesse that Alice was taken?

Chapter 6

Alicia had her grocery cart half-full before her nerves finally settled down and her pulse rate returned to normal. She stared at the packages of frozen vegetables, remembering that moment when the sheriff had walked toward them.

In an instant she'd believed that she'd lost the battle, that somehow Broderick and Ruth had not only found her, but they'd managed to get a warrant for her arrest as well.

Once again she was struck by how fragile her position was. It was a battle with one side weighed heavy with money and power. She had neither. All she had was a driving need to protect Rebecca.

She picked up several packages of frozen corn and threw them into her cart. The scare had reminded her that she and Rebecca could call no place home for too long. The only way to stay safe was to keep moving. They would remain at Cameron's ranch through the winter, but come spring they would need to find another small town in another state in which to get lost.

The constant moving, the interminable worry wasn't the kind of life she wanted for Rebecca, but the alternative was infinitely more dreadful.

Leaving would be hard. Rebecca loved it at the ranch and Alicia had to admit she'd been happy the past couple of weeks. Cameron's ranch hands were friendly and she found the vast open space surrounding Cameron's home soothing and peaceful. But, she would be a fool to allow them to get so comfortable that one of Broderick's minions found them.

She left the frozen section and headed for the canned goods, her thoughts turning to Cameron. She felt as if an explosion was imminent between them. Tension simmered in the air, barely contained whenever they were together.

He'd managed to garner pieces of her past from her, yet gave nothing of himself away. He never spoke of anything personal, never hinted at what caused the dark shadows in his eyes, the latent emotions that only shone there in unguarded moments.

Elena had mentioned something about his self-imposed cocoon of isolation. What had caused him to cut himself off from everything and everyone? He didn't appear to have many friends, at least none who had come to the ranch to see him. He was a good-looking man but no women called the house and as far as she knew he wasn't seeing anyone at all.

She sensed a tragedy in his past…something that had made him close himself off. The only time he seemed truly at ease was with Rebecca. Alicia often stood at the window in the kitchen and watched her daughter and Cameron as they worked together on Sugar. His smile came readily for Rebecca and once or twice she'd heard the robust sound of his laughter.

Alicia wished those smiles were occasionally directed at her, wished just once she'd be the recipient of or able to share in one of those moments of laughter.

She wheeled her cart around a corner and smacked into another cart. "Oh…I'm sorry!" she exclaimed, then smiled as she recognized Millicent Creighton as the owner of the cart she'd run into.

"Hello, dear," Millicent said with a wide grin. "How nice to see you again. Doing a little shopping I see." Her gaze swept the contents of Alicia's cart as if she might write a column on the eating habits of the people at the Gallagher ranch.

"Yes, and my next stop is at the discount store for a Halloween costume for Rebecca." Alicia stared at Millicent's hat, an orange felt with little white ghosts and black-clad witches around the brim.

"Will you be coming to the Halloween party at the community center this Saturday night?" Millicent asked.

"Oh, I don't know. My plans were just to take Rebecca to a couple of houses here in town for trick-or-treating then go back home."

"Oh dear, you must come to the party with your little girl. She would have a ball. The children bob for apples and play pass-the-egg while the grown-ups socialize and enjoy Bob Thurman's hot apple cider."

"It sounds like a wonderful time," Alicia agreed. "And now I'd better get the last of my groceries. I don't want Mr. Gallagher to have to wait for me."

"I hope to see you there," Millicent said as she moved her cart away from Alicia's. "Don't forget…Saturday night at the community center. The fun begins around seven." She wiggled two pudgy fingers in parting, then disappeared down an aisle.

It took Alicia another ten minutes to finish up her shopping. She'd just loaded the grocery bags into the back of the truck when Cameron appeared.

"All done?" he asked.

"Actually, I was wondering if you'd mind stopping by the discount store for just a minute. I need to pick up some things for Halloween for Rebecca."

"Okay," he agreed.

At the discount store, Cameron stayed in the truck while Alicia ran inside to purchase what she needed. For the last several days Rebecca had been talking about Halloween, that she wanted to go trick-or-treating dressed as a cowgirl.

Thankfully, cowgirl outfits seemed to be popular. Alicia found a little western hat, a pair of gold plastic spurs and a colorful kerchief. These items, added to a white blouse and a denim skirt would transform Rebecca into a little cowgirl extraordinaire.

"Let me guess," Cameron said as she got back into the truck. "Rebecca wants to be a cowgirl."

Alicia laughed. "You're absolutely right. She refused to consider anything else."

Cameron started the truck and shook his head. "She's a good kid and I think she's a natural with horses. By spring I'll have her riding as if she were born on a horse."

Alicia said nothing as she wondered where she and her daughter would be in the spring. Hopefully someplace where Rebecca could indulge her passion for horses and cowboys. Perhaps another dusty little town, this time in Wyoming.

Depression settled like a mantle across her shoulders and she focused her gaze out the window. The gray skies seemed to reflect her despair. How long would they have to run? How long would they need to hide? Would it never end? The fear? The uncertainty?

"I saw Millicent Creighton in the grocery store," she said, trying to pull herself from her melancholy.

"What did she have on her head? A caldron of bubbling witches' brew?"

Alicia laughed. "What is it with those hats of hers? Does she always wear them?"

"For as long as I've lived in Mustang. From what I understand she began wearing them soon after her husband died, around the same time that she got the job writing the social column for the *Mustang Monitor*." He grinned wryly. "Just one of many colorful characters Mustang has to offer."

"There're other colorful characters?"

A small burst of laughter left him, the sound deep and pleasant. "Mustang is full of them. For the most part Mustang is a town of misfits who have found acceptance here."

"Are you one of the misfits?"

He looked at her, his eyes dark and forbidding. "Definitely."

She sensed a warning in the single word answer, as if he were cautioning her about himself. "Millicent mentioned something about a Halloween party this Saturday night at the community center," she said.

He nodded. "About four times a year they throw a shindig. You should go, take Rebecca. The Halloween gathering is as much for the kids as the adults."

"Maybe I will," she replied. "Will you be going?"

"No." He frowned, as if the entire idea was distasteful. "I'm not into the social scene. I went to the Summerfest gathering several months ago and that was the first and last time for me."

"You don't like parties?" she asked.

His gaze was dark as he looked at her. "I don't like people."

Again Alicia had the feeling that he suffered a deep hurt, a heartache so intense it had made him pull into himself and refuse to consider allowing anyone into his private space.

They rode the rest of the way to the ranch in silence. When they got home Cameron helped her carry in the groceries then he disappeared in the direction of the corral.

As Alicia put away the groceries, she found herself constantly drawn to the window, where she had a view of Cameron in the corral with the horse he'd been attempting to gentle.

He stood in the center of the wooden enclosure, a hand stretched out toward the horse, who pawed the ground and pranced nervously before him.

It was amazing to Alicia that a man who displayed little patience in general, would exhibit so much patience with his horses and with Rebecca.

''I don't like people.'' His words rang in her ears as she remembered the deep shadows that had darkened his eyes. A suggestion of hurt, a whisper of pain, she wondered what exactly had put those shadows in his eyes.

''Go to him,'' she whispered aloud, urging the horse to trust him, to reward his patience.

Go to him. How she wished she could do just that, somehow hold him in her arms, kiss away the pain she sensed he carried deep within his soul.

She whirled away from the window. Foolish thoughts. What good would it do to somehow manage to heal his wounds if she eventually intended to leave? There was no future here for her. Her life here was based on half-truths and protective lies and eventually she and Rebecca would have to pick up and find another place to live a life of lies.

At the moment, she saw no future, no stability, no happily-ever-after for either her daughter or herself. As long as Broderick and Ruth had breath in their bodies, Rebecca and Alicia would continue to run.

"Mommy, do I look like a real cowgirl?" Rebecca spun around, displaying her Halloween outfit for Alicia's approval.

"You look exactly like a real cowgirl," Alicia replied with an indulgent smile.

Rebecca walked across the bedroom, plastic spurs whirling. "And I sound like a real cowgirl, too. Don't I?"

Alicia laughed. "You do, indeed," she agreed, even though the spurs were attached to plain white tennis shoes.

"Come on, Mommy. Let's go!"

"Just a minute. I'm almost ready," Alicia replied as she gave her appearance a final check in her dresser mirror. She gave her hair a final flick with the brush, pleased that in the last month it had grown enough to finally take on a more natural shape. She'd had to color it again to hide the pale roots, but she was finally getting used to the dark color.

"Now can we go?" Rebecca asked with scarcely hidden impatience.

Alicia set the brush down and nodded. "Now we can go," she agreed. She had decided to take Rebecca and go to the Halloween party at the community center. Rebecca had insisted that all her friends from school would be there and she'd promised her friends she would be there as well.

Rebecca scurried down the stairs ahead of Alicia, chattering like a magpie about the party. "Jessica

said they have lots of candy and all the kids play
fun games,'' she exclaimed. ''Hi, Mr. Lallagher,''
she said as Cameron appeared at the foot of the
stairs.

He frowned. ''Excuse me…I don't believe I know
you, little Ms. Cowgirl. Have you seen my friend
Rebecca?'' he asked. ''I have a surprise for her.''

Rebecca giggled. ''Mr. Lallagher, it's me! I'm
Rebecca.''

Cameron's features emitted surprise and Rebecca's giggles increased. ''Why, Rebecca, I didn't
recognize you,'' he said. He held out a box to her.

Alicia smiled at him, loving the sound of her
daughter's childish merriment. He looked handsome
as sin, clad in a tight pair of worn jeans and a white
shirt that emphasized his sun-bronzed features. She
felt a familiar heat sweep through her and quickly
averted her gaze from him and to her daughter.

Rebecca opened the box and gasped in stunned
surprise. ''Oh…oh Mommy, look.'' She held up a
pair of miniature red cowboy boots, the image of
horses tooled into the polished leather.

''I didn't know for sure what size,'' Cameron
said, looking ill-at-ease. ''I told Gus they were for
a six-year-old and so he guessed at the size.''

''They fit. I know they do,'' Rebecca said as she
sat down and tugged off her tennis shoes. As Rebecca pulled on the new boots, a wave of desire
struck Alicia. She looked at Cameron, speechless for
a moment. With his passion he could seduce her
body, but with this sort of kindness, he could own
her very soul.

"I told you they fit," Rebecca exclaimed as she stood. "Now I'm a real real cowgirl." Without warning she launched herself at Cameron. He caught her and she wrapped her arms around his neck. "Thank you, Mr. Lallagher," Rebecca said as she kissed him soundly on the cheek.

"Tennis shoes aren't appropriate for Montana," Cameron said, his gruff tone letting Alicia know he was embarrassed by Rebecca's effusive show of affection.

"Come on, sweetheart. It's time to get to the party," Alicia said.

"I'll drive you," Cameron said. Alicia looked at him in surprise. "I figured I might as well go, if for nothing else than to please my sister who doesn't think I socialize enough."

Moments later the three of them were in Cameron's pickup heading into town. Rebecca sat between Cameron and Alicia, alternating her attention from one to the other.

"Jessica said we'll play games and the grown-ups dance at the party. I like to dance. Sometimes me and Jessica dance at recess. Jessica said I'd get lots of candy tonight at the party," she said to Cameron. "I could share my candy with you, Mr. Lallagher."

"That's very nice of you," Cameron returned. "Who is this Jessica?"

"Jessica is my bestest friend," Rebecca replied.

"Jessica Hopkins," Alicia explained.

Cameron nodded. "That must be Roger Hopkins's youngest."

"I've spoken to Mrs. Hopkins several times on the phone. She seems quite nice," Alicia said.

"They're a good, solid family."

Rebecca looked at Cameron curiously. "How come you don't have a family?"

Alicia saw Cameron's hands tighten on the steering wheel. "Little Miss Big Nose, you shouldn't ask personal questions," she admonished Rebecca gently.

"No, it's all right," Cameron replied. "I guess I just got used to being alone."

Rebecca touched his hand lightly. "You don't got to be alone anymore. Now me and Mommy will be your pretend family."

Cameron gave a curt nod. Thankfully at that moment he turned into the parking lot of the community center and Rebecca's attention shifted to the little ghosts and goblins who approached the building in the company of their parents.

The interior of the community center had been decorated for the holiday. Orange and black crepe paper hung from the ceiling and bales of hay were stacked to provide casual seating. Rebecca immediately spied a group of her friends from school and with a nod from Alicia ran to join them.

"Please don't feel obligated to stay with me just because we rode together," Alicia said to Cameron as he guided her toward a row of folding chairs against one wall.

"I never feel obligated to anyone," he answered as she sat. "Perhaps you'd rather I leave you alone?"

"No, not at all." She felt a blush warm her cheeks. "I really don't know anyone else here. I...I would enjoy your company." Her blush intensified.

He sat next to her and folded his arms across his chest. If body language meant anything, Alicia recognized he was closed off, isolating himself despite the crowd around them.

"That was very kind...buying the boots for Rebecca," she said.

He shrugged. "She needed a pair of boots if she's going to muck around in the stables."

"Don't worry, Cameron. I won't tell anyone you did something nice for my daughter," Alicia said dryly. "I wouldn't want to mess up your reputation as a tough man."

Before Cameron had a chance to reply, Millicent Creighton appeared. "Alice...I'm so glad you decided to come to our little gathering." Clad in a black dress and wearing a traditional witch's hat, Millicent smiled broadly at Alicia. "Come with me, dear, and let me introduce you to some of Mustang's finest."

Alicia looked helplessly at Cameron as Millicent took her hand and pulled her up from her chair.

"Oh, don't worry about Cameron," Millicent exclaimed. "He's used to being alone at these parties."

For the next hour, Millicent dragged Alicia from group to group, introducing her to all the townspeople Alicia hadn't yet met.

As Alicia visited with the various people Millicent introduced her to, she was aware of Cameron's gaze following her, lingering on her.

She remembered the night when he'd come home from the Roundup, those moments when his hand had touched her hair, caressed the side of her face and a renewed burst of heat filled her.

Again she had the feeling that sooner or later an eruption would occur between them, an explosion of physical desire and aching need. Sooner or later she was going to have to decide what she intended to do when the explosion occurred.

Cameron shifted position on the hard chair, wondering what madness had prompted him to come. And yet, deep inside he knew the madness, and it had a name. Alice.

He watched her as she talked with a group of people, noticed several of the single men in the room also watching her with interest. And that's why he'd come.

He wasn't sure when it had happened, when he'd begun to think of her as his. Maybe it had begun that day he'd talked to Jesse Wilder and staked his claim. He suspected it had begun even before then, as early as the moment he had first seen her standing on his porch.

He'd had no intention of coming until he'd seen Alicia dressed for the night. Wearing a short, dark blue dress that emphasized the length of her shapely legs and intensified the blue of her eyes, she looked prettier than he'd ever seen her.

There was no way he'd sit at home and let all the

other single men of Mustang pursue her. Mustang never had enough eligible women, and he wanted to make certain that the bachelors of the town knew Alice wasn't available.

Cameron was aware of the dichotomy of his feelings where Alice was concerned. He didn't want her in his life, but he definitely wanted her in his bed. He didn't want a commitment for more than a night or two.

He wasn't fit for any woman for a long-term investment. As long as Alice understood that, there would be no problems and no false hopes, no disappointment and no expectations.

He tensed as he saw Sam Davidson, the bartender from the Roundup move in Alice's direction. Sam was a good-looking man, a smooth operator who had a weakness for pretty women and an aversion to fidelity.

Cameron stood and stalked toward Alice, intent on impeding whatever carnal thoughts Sam might have about the woman. The band had begun and he had a feeling Sam intended to ask Alice to dance.

Cameron reached her side mere seconds after Sam. "Evening, Sam." He cupped Alice's elbow with his hand, a distinctly proprietorial gesture. "I thought maybe you might be ready for some cider," he said to Alice.

She nodded, her eyes registering surprise. "That sounds wonderful," she agreed. She smiled at Sam, who had backed away beneath Cameron's unflinching stare. "Perhaps a later dance," she said, confirming Cameron's suspicion that Sam had asked her to dance.

Cameron led her to the table in the corner that held a variety of drinks. He ladled her a cup of the hot spiced cider, then got himself one.

As they sipped the spicy hot drink they stood at the edge of the dance area, watching it fill with couples. "I'm glad we came," Alice said. She smiled at him, the smile creating a familiar heat inside Cameron. "Everyone has been so nice and I'm having a wonderful time."

It showed. Her eyes sparkled and an attractive flush colored her cheeks. The heat inside Cameron intensified as he imagined the way her eyes would glow as he made love to her. He took another drink of the cider, telling himself it was the drink that heated his insides and had nothing to do with the woman standing next to him.

He followed her gaze as it swept around the room, apparently seeking her daughter. Rebecca stood on the opposite side of the room with a bunch of her friends, giggling as they watched the grown-ups dancing. His heart softened as Rebecca's gaze connected with his and she gave him a wide smile and waved a hand.

He returned the wave, felt a blush warm his face as Alice caught his gesture. She frowned thoughtfully. "I'm a little worried about how close Rebecca is getting to you."

He looked at her in surprise. "Why?"

She shrugged and looked into her half-empty cup. "She's had so many losses recently. I don't want her to come to depend on you being a part of her life and later be hurt.''

"Hurt is a part of life. It's what makes you strong,'' he countered.

Her gaze held his for a long moment. "I disagree,'' she replied softly. "Hurt makes you scared, makes you reluctant to put your heart on the line again.''

Cameron didn't like the turn of topic. It hit too close to home and he refused to believe himself scared of anything or anyone. Besides, she was wrong. Hurt didn't make you scared, it made you smart.

"Cameron...Ms. Burwell.'' Jesse Wilder approached them. Clad in his sheriff's uniform he looked ready to arrest the first partier who got out of line. "Nice to see you both here,'' he said.

"You on duty?'' Cameron asked.

Jesse grinned, unpinned his badge and tucked it into his pocket. "Officially I got off duty ten minutes ago. Thought I'd stop by and join in the fun.'' He smiled at Alice. "How about giving the local sheriff a twirl around the dance floor?''

For a moment Cameron thought she would decline, then she threw her empty cup in a nearby trash container and nodded her assent to Jesse.

Cameron watched darkly as the two moved to the dance floor. Once again he sought his chair and sank down, his gaze following the movement of Alice's hips as she danced to the beat of the music.

For the next hour he watched as Alice danced with first one, then another of the men of Mustang.

Her graceful movements and seemingly natural rhythm made her a joy to watch, although Cameron suspected he would have found her easy on the eyes even if she'd been clumsy and suffered a lack of rhythm.

Still, watching her was torture, sweet torture. The sway of her hips hypnotized him and the length of her legs taunted him. He wanted everything from her...and nothing. She angered him by stirring forgotten emotions, awakening suppressed desire.

When she finally rejoined him, she sank into the chair next to him with an exhausted sigh. "Whew. I can't remember when I've danced so much." She raised her hair from her neck, exposing damp tendrils that clung to her skin.

Cameron frowned irritably. At that moment Rebecca ran over to where they sat. "Mommy, Jessica asked me to spend the night with her, and her mommy said it would be okay. Please, please? I got my fingers crossed that you'll say yes." She paused to draw a deep breath.

"Oh, honey. I don't think..." Alice began, then paused as Jessica's mother, Marianne Hopkins and Jessica approached them.

"We'd love to have Rebecca spend the night," Marianne said. "I promise we'd have her back home first thing in the morning."

"Please, Mrs. Burwell," Jessica pleaded.

"Please, Mommy," Rebecca added. "I got my fingers double, double crossed!"

Alice laughed and held out her hands in defeat. "How can I say no to double, double crossed?"

Rebecca and Jessica whooped and hollered their excitement as Alice and Marianne made the final arrangements.

As Marianne and the two girls went back across the room where her husband awaited them, Alice turned and stared at Cameron.

He knew the moment she realized what he had already discerned…that this night would be the first night they were in the house together…alone.

Chapter 7

They rode home in silence. The clouds had blown away, leaving a perfect half-moon to shine down to earth. Although Alicia's gaze was directed out the window, she was intensely aware of Cameron. His scent drifted around her, his vibrating energy filled the cab of the pickup.

Without Rebecca to serve as a buffer between them, Alicia's senses seemed heightened where Cameron was concerned. She'd felt his gaze on her all night long. Dark and brooding, so intense she felt as if he were able to peer beneath her clothing, peek beneath her flesh to the heart and soul within.

And if he saw her heart, then he knew her desire. She could no longer fool herself. She wanted Cameron Gallagher. She wanted his arms around her, his warm skin against her own. She wanted his lips on hers as he moved intimately against her, inside her.

She shifted uncomfortably, changing positions as if to do so would change her thoughts.

"Tired?" His deep voice broke the silence as he pulled up before the ranch.

She started to say yes, but knew it would be a lie. "Not really. To tell the truth, I'm kind of wired." Wired wasn't the word. She was tense, nervous and expectant.

"Yeah, me too," he said as they got out of the truck.

Again silence prevailed as they walked from the truck to the house. She knew she should go directly to her room, close the door and get a good night's sleep. And yet she didn't want to go to her room. "You want me to make some coffee?" she asked.

"No." He stood before her, his eyes glowing with an almost predatory light that stole her breath. He moved closer to her, so close she could feel the warmth of his breath on her face. "Coffee isn't what I want."

Her own breath ached in her chest, momentarily trapped there by the hunger that sparked in his eyes. "What do you want?" The words tumbled softly from her lips.

"You."

The single word, combined with the heat of his gaze shot shivers up her spine. A little voice warned her not to be a fool, that a night with Cameron would only be just that…a single night. And yet isn't that what makes it so perfect, a louder inner voice exclaimed. After all, she couldn't offer him a future even if he wanted one.

Just one night. A night to remember. A night of being nothing more than a woman to this man.

He seemed to sense her silent acquiescence. His arms wound around her as he lowered his head to claim her lips with his own.

Fire leapt in her veins as his mouth moved ravenously against hers. His kiss stole her capacity to think, transported her to a place where only physical sensation was possible.

She felt his kiss throughout her body, the heat suffusing her from head to toe. She tasted the subtle flavors of apples and cinnamon, but didn't know if it was from the spiced apple cider she had drank or the cup he'd enjoyed. In any case, it didn't matter.

As the kiss deepened and his tongue swirled around hers, she lost all thought of the dance they had attended. The four walls of the living room faded into nothingness. There was only this moment and this man.

His hands splayed across her back and caressed up across her shoulder blades, then down to her lower back. Electricity followed in their wake, heating the skin beneath her dress with evocative warmth.

His lips left hers and traveled toward her ear. ''I want you to be sure,'' he whispered.

''I am,'' she whispered, then shivered again as he nuzzled her earlobe.

His hands slid down to cup her buttocks and she gasped as he pulled her into him, against his hardness. His obvious desire for her heightened her passion.

Robert had never looked at her with greedy eyes, he'd never kissed her as if he were starving and she was the last morsel of food left on earth. But Cameron…sweet Cameron made her want ache deep inside her. He made her want to be everything to him.

His lips found hers again, burning with intensity, drawing breath from her and giving it back. As they kissed, his hands once again clutched her buttocks and his fingers moved, working her dress up around her hips. He moaned as the fabric gave way and he touched the slick silk of her panty hose.

Alicia moved her hands across the width of his back, felt the play of his muscles as they bunched beneath her touch. Strong…so very strong. In his embrace she felt safe, as if nothing could ever harm her again. She reveled in the feeling, wanted to lose herself completely in him.

"I want you in my bed." Without waiting for her reply, he swept her up into his arms as if she weighed no more than Rebecca.

As he carried her up the stairs, she thought of his room, his bed, how many times over the past few weeks she'd neatly arranged his sheets and blankets, and imagined herself tangled with him in them.

She buried her face in the hollow of his neck, breathing in the scent of him, the tantalizing mixture of earthy cologne, the late autumn wind and utter maleness. She spied a pulse beating at the base of his throat and pressed her lips against it.

He gasped and nearly stumbled. His arms tightened around her. "Damn, woman. You have no idea what you do to me," he growled.

"Show me," she said, surprising herself with her own brazenness.

He paused midstep and looked down at her, his eyes twin infernos. "Let me get you upstairs and I'll show you…unless you prefer to finish this right here on the stairs?" One of his dark eyebrows quirked upward, making him look both teasing and sexy at the same time. "So what will it be? My bed or the stairs?"

"Your bed," she replied. "And hurry."

Her heart pounded with wild anticipation as he took the last of the stairs two at a time. She felt as if every moment of every day since she'd met him had simply been foreplay in preparation of this night. At the top of the stairs he flipped on the hall light.

She didn't think it possible, but the beating of her heart increased when he entered his bedroom. Her throat felt dry and scratchy and she knew it was the first stir of nervousness.

It had been over a year since she'd made love with any man and Robert had been her first and only. She had a feeling Cameron's expectations would be quite different, that unlike Robert, Cameron's appetite would be voracious and he might find her relative inexperience uninspiring.

Cameron gave her no time to entertain further doubts and nerves. He lay her on the bed and joined her there, his mouth once again finding hers as if he couldn't get enough of the taste of her.

As he kissed her, his fingers worked the buttons that ran up the front of her dress, nimbly unfastening

each one. She did the same to his shirt, wanting…needing to feel his naked chest, wanting…needing to tangle her fingers in the springy
dark hair that grew there.

She finished with his shirt buttons at the same
time he unfastened the last of the buttons on her
dress. Gently, as if unwrapping a precious package,
he opened her dress, allowing the material to fall to
either side of her, exposing her bra, panty hose and
panties to the naked heat of his gaze.

In turn, she sat up and peeled his shirt from his
shoulders, pushing it off to bare his broad chest. In
the faint spill of light from the hallway, his skin
gleamed bronze, looking eminently touchable. She
leaned forward and pressed her lips against his flesh,
felt his swift intake of breath at her intimate touch.

Cameron leaned forward and pulled her against
him, her chest against his as his hands went behind
her and unsnapped her lacy bra. The wispy material
fell into his hands. He tossed it aside and covered
her breasts with his palms.

Alicia closed her eyes, responding to his touch as
if his hands were electric sockets conducting power
through her. She heard herself moan, the sound deep
and throaty as he captured a nipple between two
fingers. Tingles of pleasure coursed through her as
his hands worked magic.

With Robert, making love had always been quick
and accomplished in the dark. Cameron seemed to
be in no hurry. He touched her face, smoothed fingers over her collarbones, captured her breasts once
again in the warmth of his palms.

He acted as if they had all of eternity to complete the act and Alicia's desire climbed to uncharted new heights.

She was the one who took off her panty hose, then grasped the waistband of his jeans and plucked impatiently. He laughed, an indulgent deep rumble that reverberated in the pit of her stomach. ''Patience, sweet Alice,'' he said, but patience wasn't what she saw shining from his eyes.

Within minutes he'd slid out of his jeans, exposing a pair of cotton briefs and the evidence of a desire impossible to deny. She slid a leg across his, reveling in the feel of his dark hair against the silken smoothness of her own.

He was so utterly male, so undeniably masculine and being in his arms made her feel more female than she'd ever felt in her life. She never would have guessed him a gentle man, but each caress was accompanied by a kiss. His hands, although the hands of a rancher, calloused and weatherworn, touched her with infinite tenderness.

And in his touch, in each of his kisses, she saw his heart. Not the hard soul he presented to the world, but the heart of the inner man he kept so tightly controlled. A man she suspected capable of great emotion and tremendous sensitivity.

By the time he removed her panties, she felt as if her entire body was a single nerve singing the energy of mindless desire. And when he removed his underwear she touched him there...where he throbbed and ached, loving the sounds he made as she stroked him. When he rose to cover her, she pushed him back and smiled. "Patience, sweet Cameron," she whispered, and was rewarded by his burst of laughter.

The laughter lasted only a moment, then they became a tangle of arms and legs, a flurry of kisses and caresses. Alicia felt herself melting away, drifting on a cloud of unimaginable pleasure.

This was what it was supposed to be, she thought with what little rational mind was left. This is what the movies talk about, what inspires poets to write. This was what she had never had before. Tears sprang to her eyes as she gave silent thanks that at least this once she was experiencing this kind of wild, euphoric desire.

She cried out in pleasure as he entered her. For a moment he remained still, as if savoring the feel of her. In that single moment of unity, Alicia knew completeness, knew nothing she'd ever experienced with Robert had come close to this kind of absolute wholeness.

He moved against her and she arched up to meet him, their movements becoming more frenzied as he stroked her deep and hard. She clutched at his back, then wrapped her legs around him and eagerly drew him inside her.

He pulsated within her, his mouth finding hers in a kiss that stole her breath. He owned her. As his body possessed hers, he owned her heart. She tangled her hands in his hair, then clutched again at his back, half-crazed as he carried her higher and higher.

And then she was there, tumbling over the precipice, plunging into a place void of feelings, fraught with sensation. She cried his name as she rode the crest of the waves of pleasure. Tears once again burned her eyes, slipped down her cheeks as she realized she wanted this night to last forever. She wanted to be in his arms for a lifetime.

He stiffened against her as he reached his peak. ''Alice,'' he cried and in that moment reality slammed back into her. There would be no forever. Her name wasn't Alice and she had no lifetime to offer him.

Cameron awoke just before dawn. He turned over in bed, seeking the warmth of Alice, but she was gone. Her pillow still held the imprint of her head and when he placed his hand where she'd been, he felt the residual heat from her body.

He sat up, raked a hand through his hair and moved his shoulders, the last of his sleep falling away. He cocked his head and caught the faint sound of the shower running. Instantly his mind filled with a vision of her standing beneath a hot spray of water. And just as quickly his desire returned as if it hadn't been sated only hours before.

He'd envisioned what making love to Alice would be like for the past four weeks, but nothing in his imagination had prepared him for the reality. She'd been far more passionate than he'd ever dreamed. She'd given as well as received, lost herself completely in the act. It had been an incredible experience, one he wanted to repeat.

Before allowing misgivings to enter his mind, he

got out of bed and padded to the bathroom. Steamy warmth and the scent of strawberries greeted him as he opened the bathroom door. He stepped into the thick vapor and closed the door behind him.

He paused a brief moment, wondering if she would welcome his company beneath the shower spray. Without allowing doubts to halt him, he slid open the glass shower door.

She whirled around and faced him, eyes wide in surprise. Hair slicked back and without a single dab of makeup, she looked as beautiful as he'd ever seen her.

"I thought you might like your back scrubbed," he said, his voice husky as he drank in the vision of her.

She didn't answer, but handed him a loofah sponge and presented him her back. He stepped into the enclosure and pulled the door tightly closed.

The sponge smelled of sun-ripened strawberries and he realized it was some kind of body wash she used. He squeezed some of the red gel onto the sponge and swirled it across her back. Back and forth, up and down, he was mesmerized by the action.

He heard her breath quicken as his caresses encircled her upper ribs, flirting with the sides of her breasts. His own breath escaped on a ragged sigh as he moved closer to her. His body pressed against hers and the warm cascade of water washed over them.

She leaned back against him, moaning softly as he moved the loofah across one breast and then the other. He dipped his head forward and kissed her shoulder, the skin impossibly silky beneath his lips.

He moved his hips back and forth against her buttocks, the friction creating an explosive need inside him. He moved back from her, wanting control and afraid of losing it too quickly.

Turning in his arms, she raised her face to him and his lips sought hers. As they kissed, she reached down and grasped him, her hands slippery with sweet-smelling suds. The sensation of the water, the taste of her mouth against his and her hand enclosing around him nearly undid him.

"Not yet," he whispered against her neck. "Not until I've tasted every inch of you." Her eyes flared at his words and her pupils dilated with desire. Her hand fell away and she leaned weakly against the side of the shower.

He began at her mouth, plying it with heat, then moved to her shoulders…her collarbones…and down to her breasts. He used his mouth, his tongue and little nips of his teeth to evoke whimpers of pleasure from her. He dropped the forgotten sponge on the floor, preferring to use his hands to smooth across her soft skin.

From her breasts he kissed down the flat of her abdomen, working from one side to the other to taste each place where he felt a rib.

Her moans increased in intensity, feeding him with their erotic sounds. She tossed her head from side to side, her eyes narrowed and turned a deep shade of blue.

Her pubic hair was pale, attesting to her true col-

oring and he rubbed across the core of her sexuality
with a single finger. She cried out and arched her
back, as if urging him on.

He needed no prodding. He continued caressing,
touching, tasting, wanting to possess her as no man
ever had before. Her pleasure became his. Each of
her moans evoked one of his own. It was as if they
were a single body and he lost track of where she
ended and he began. He felt her climax approaching
and increased the fervor of his caresses, wondrous
at how completely she gave herself to him. She held
nothing back and as she tumbled over the edge, she
cried his name again and again.

He entered her, slid into her tight heat and felt
the last of his control slip away. Her muscles tightened around him, as if seeking to keep him trapped
inside her forever. They moved like lovers well accustomed to each other, fitting together with a per-
fection Cameron had never known.

With the steam surrounding them, he felt cut off
from the rest of the world, transported to a place
where there was only Alice…sweet-smelling, sweet-
tasting Alice.

He felt the end approaching, felt himself swelling
with the approach of it. He wanted her with him and
he picked her up, allowing her to wrap her legs
around his waist while he remained buried deep
within her.

In this position, he dipped his head forward and
captured one of her erect, pink nipples with his
mouth. Her entire body grew taut and he knew by
the glaze of her eyes, the moan that began deep in

her throat that she was there. He closed his eyes and let go, felt their simultaneous completion sweep over them.

As she once again cried his name again and again, he felt a small piece of his heart...a piece that had been ice-cold for so long warm and melt away.

He held her until their breathing had returned to normal, until the cascade of water turned tepid, portending the end of the heated water in the tank. Only then did he set her feet back on the ground and smile. "Now that's how to take a shower."

She smiled, but he sensed her sudden shyness and an awkward moment of silence sprang between them. He stepped out of the shower stall. "I'll see you downstairs," he said, then slid the door closed.

He grabbed a thick towel and wrapped it around his waist, then left the bathroom, knowing she would prefer to dry and dress without his company.

He dressed quickly, pulling on a pair of his work jeans and a thick flannel shirt. As he buttoned the shirt he moved to the window, where dawn was just beginning to break, lighting the eastern sky with pink and gold.

Dawn's light brought with it a small ration of regret. For the past three weeks he'd wanted Alice, and he'd hoped by making love to her the wanting would ease. But it hadn't. Even now, fully sated thoughts of her stirred him.

He went downstairs and started the coffee, refusing to dwell on her or his own regrets. They'd had their night together, and a bonus round this morning. It should be enough.

He was seated at the table sipping fresh brew when she entered the kitchen. Her cheeks pinkened as her gaze met his, but her smile was soft…an intimate smile for him alone.

"Are you hungry?" she asked.

He shook his head and gestured to his mug. "This is fine."

She poured herself a cup and sank into the chair across from him. Again an awkward silence rose up, creating tension that filled the room. She laughed self-consciously, breaking the silence. "This is hard, isn't it? I'm not sure what to say to you…how to act."

"I suppose we act like we have every other morning you've been here," he replied. "Nothing's changed. Not really." He heard the defensive edge in his own voice.

She eyed him wryly. "Don't worry Cameron, I don't expect anything from you. I remember…no promises, no commitments and it suits me just fine. In fact, I wouldn't have it any other way."

For some reason her words irritated him. "What? You like me well enough to sleep with, but not well enough for anything else?"

She studied him thoughtfully. "I don't know you well enough for anything else. You're a difficult man to get to know, Cameron Gallagher."

He shrugged. "What do you want to know?"

She sipped her coffee, her gaze not wavering from his. She placed her cup back in her saucer. "Did you always want to be a rancher?"

He nodded and smiled. "I'm kind of like Rebecca. I knew I wanted to be a cowboy from the time I was a small child.''

She leaned forward, her eyes glowing with warmth as if she were enjoying a peek into his past. ''Did you grow up on a ranch?''

''No. When I was seventeen my parents moved from Detroit to Billings and it was then I got my first real taste of ranch life.''

''You mentioned before that your father was dead. What about your mother? Is she still alive?''

A sharp pain pierced through him. ''She died with my father in the plane accident.'' The pain intensified as he thought of the months just before their death. Still grieving for Ginny, still reeling with Samuel's betrayal, Cameron had closed himself off from everyone, lost precious moments with his parents.

''Cameron, I'm so sorry.'' Alice's hand covered his, warm and soft and sweetly comforting.

He stood, jerking his hand from hers. ''I'd better get to the chores. The morning will be gone before we know it.''

He didn't want her comforting touch, and he didn't want her peeks into his past. She didn't need to know him, just as he didn't care about her. They'd been bed partners for a night. Nothing more.

Not waiting for her reply, not wanting to even look at her, he grabbed a work jacket and his hat from the coat tree then left the kitchen through the backdoor.

The early morning air was cold, so cold he could see his breath. He shoved his hands in his pockets and headed for the corral. The horse inside backed into the far corner, as far away from Cameron as the wooden confines would allow.

Damn, she was stubborn, refusing to trust him. Within the next couple of days he'd need to move her inside. The weather was definitely taking a turn toward winter and in Montana snow could come without much warning.

He watched the horse, pawing the ground, ears twitching nervously and his thoughts strayed to Alice. As he thought of their lovemaking, he came to a painful conclusion.

His love for Ginny hadn't been the right kind for two people planning a lifetime together. He'd loved Ginny as he loved Elena. It had been a protective love, but devoid of the kind of passion that swelled in him with thoughts of Alice. As the fantasy of his memories fell away, leaving only stark reality, he felt bereft and empty.

Chapter 8

Alicia stood at the kitchen window, staring out at the dismal, gray skies. The weather had taken a turn for the worse. Although there had been no snow yet, the temperatures had dropped below freezing and the sun hadn't been seen all week.

She turned her gaze toward Cameron and Rebecca. Cameron was showing Rebecca how to brush and curry a horse. Sugar, the small gentle mare, stood patiently beneath the little girl's ministrations. Every few minutes Rebecca turned and smiled at Cameron and he'd return her smiles with ones of his own.

A week. It had been a full seven days since she and Cameron had made love. And since that night and early morning, he had become more distant than ever with her. He arose each morning before her and left for chores. He rarely joined her for lunch and even though the three of them shared the evening meal, he kept to himself, rarely speaking and then only to Rebecca.

Although she tried to tell herself it was better this way, better that she remember she was his house-keeper, not his lover, she couldn't help but wish for something more. And she knew her wishes were the dreams of fools.

Not a single day passed that she didn't wonder if Broderick had somehow discovered where she and Rebecca lived. Not a single day passed that she didn't worry about their future.

Her stash of money in her dresser drawer was growing…but oh, so slowly. If the time came when she'd have to fight Broderick and Ruth in a court of law she'd need a hundred times the amount in her drawer for the fight to be even close to fair.

She turned away from the window as the phone rang, an unaccustomed noise in the house. There had only been about half a dozen times the phone had rung in the time she'd been here and then only two of the calls had been for Cameron, the rest of them had been for her. Elena had called twice to visit, and Marianne Hopkins had called to discuss school activities.

"Hello?" she said when she picked up the receiver.

Silence greeted her. Not the complete silence of a dead line, but rather the quiet whisper of somebody listening…breathing.

"Hello?" she repeated, wondering if perhaps she was about to be assaulted by an obscene caller.

An audible click was her reply. She held the receiver for a long moment, sudden chills racing up and down her spine.

Had Broderick finally found them? Had she made a mistake? Somehow left a trail? Had the phone call been one of his subordinates confirming that she lived here?

She replaced the receiver into the cradle, telling herself not to jump to conclusions. ''It was just a wrong number,'' she said, as if saying the words aloud would make them true.

Even though the phone remained silent for the rest of the afternoon, Alicia continued to be on edge, her thoughts playing games of ''what if'' where she was always the loser and the price she paid was her daughter.

By the time dinner arrived and the three of them sat down to eat, she knew she was on the verge of an emotional explosion. In the weeks she and Rebecca had been running Alicia hadn't had time to mourn all that she had lost. The material world she'd left behind had been the most easily lost. Her dreams of loving support from family were the most difficult, and it was this she now felt, the loss of all her dreams.

''Rebecca, eat those peas,'' she said.

''But, Mommy, I really, really don't like them,'' Rebecca replied.

''Don't argue with me, Rebecca. Just do as I say,'' Alicia snapped, her voice loud and strident.

Rebecca's eyes instantly filled with tears and her lower lip trembled with hurt. Alicia's eyes burned with tears of her own and she quickly excused herself from the table and escaped the house through the backdoor.

The evening air was far too cold to be out without a jacket, but Alicia didn't care. She needed the bracing air to clear her head, to shiver away the nagging fear that had worried her all day.

Tears trekked down her cheeks as she thought of the look on her daughter's face. Alicia had never been one to lose her temper with Rebecca. Rebecca was accustomed to gentle rebukes, stern reminders, but not temper snaps. Alicia knew Rebecca didn't like peas…and in any case a few bites of vegetables didn't really matter.

She knew her uncharacteristic harshness with Rebecca had been a result of the fear that had gnawed at her since the phone call. She also knew it had been the consequence of her hours of mourning, of self-pity.

She heard the backdoor open and close, sensed Cameron moving to stand just behind her. "Where's Rebecca?" she asked as she quickly swiped at her tears.

"I told her she could go to her room and play." He moved even closer, so close she could feel his body heat radiating toward her. "She ate her peas."

Tears once again appeared, blurring her vision. She felt as if all the emotions she'd shoved deep inside since Robert's death were now precariously close to the surface.

Cameron's hands gripped her shoulders and he turned her around to face him. "It isn't like you to yell at Rebecca. You want to tell me what's going on? You've been tense all evening.''

"Nothing is going on." She couldn't look at him, instead stared at the scuffed toes of his cowboy boots through a veil of tears.

He placed a finger beneath her chin and forced her head up, her gaze to his. With his thumb he wiped her tears, his expression more gentle than she'd ever seen. "What's going on, Alice? Who are you running from?"

"Nobody…nothing. I—I don't know what you're talking about."

His eyes appeared to usurp the evening light, shining with a golden glow. She wanted to melt into him, snuggle against him and tell him about her fear of losing Rebecca.

"Alice, you know I'd never do anything to harm you or Rebecca. Trust me. You know you can."

Oh, how she wished she could. But she was afraid…so afraid to trust anyone. Even Cameron. She forced a light burst of laughter. "Cameron, you're making far too much of this. I had a bad day, I snapped at Rebecca. I'll go up and apologize to her and everything will be fine. That's all there is to it, nothing more."

He continued to look at her for a long moment. She could tell by his expression that he didn't believe her, but she simply couldn't risk telling him the truth. The price was too high. "Come on. You'd better get inside. It's much too cold out here." He moved his hands up and down her arms, as if to generate soothing warmth.

It worked, although the heat he created was less
a result of his present caresses and more an outcome
of the memory of his lovemaking. Her eyes must
have communicated her thoughts, for his darkened
and she heard his swift intake of breath.

She raised her lips, willing his to take her, knowing that as long as he held her, kissed her she would
feel safe. He did her bidding, his lips capturing hers
with fiery intent. He pulled her against him roughly
as if angry at her...or perhaps angry with himself.

His mouth plundered hers. His tongue swirled
around hers in an erotic dance of passion and pleasure. Alicia wound her arms around him, tangled her
fingers in the hair at his nape.

The cold evening air fell away, banished by the
warmth of his body pressed against her. The chill of
her fear ebbed as well.

All too quickly the kiss ended and he stepped
back from her. His eyes were dark and hooded. ''I
won't allow you to hide from me, Alice. Something
isn't right with your life. You've got secrets...or
problems. Fine. But don't use me as a momentary
respite from them.''

He turned and stalked back into the house. Alicia
stared after him. He was right. She had used him to
still her fears, had wanted to hide in him. But, what
he didn't know, couldn't know is what she was just
beginning to realize. If she wasn't careful...very
careful, she'd find herself in love with Cameron Gallagher.

Cameron walked back into the house, irritated by
her...and by his own thoughts. Damn, he thought

he knew what he wanted from Alice…a night or two of passion spent, a sharing of mutual lust. But when she'd run out the backdoor, when he'd seen the tears sparkling in her lovely eyes, he'd wanted more from her than a mere physical intimacy.

He'd wanted to know what made her cry. And he suddenly wanted to be the one to always dry her tears. And it had been that that had created his irritation with her.

Damn her, for pulling him back to life. Damn her for making him wonder about her, making him care about her. He wasn't sure when the knowledge that she was running from somebody had hit him, but he knew his suspicions couldn't be far from the truth.

The stories she'd told that didn't exactly jibe. Her nervousness when Jesse approached, her adamant refusal to allow Millicent to mention her presence here in the paper.

All of these things had combined in his head to create an indisputable truth and no denial from her convinced him otherwise. She was afraid. She was on the run, and for the first time in two years, he wanted to help somebody. He wanted to help Alice.

He walked through the kitchen and into the living room. It had been Rebecca first who had managed to pierce through the protective shield he'd erected around his emotions. Rebecca with her sunny smile and love for all things cowboyish.

Sinking onto the sofa, he raked a hand through his hair. Yes, Rebecca had initially pierced the shield and he felt naked, vulnerable without it.

Why didn't Alice trust him? It irked him that she could lie in his arms, make passionate love with him, and yet refuse to bare the secrets she harbored.

"You're a difficult man to get to know, Cameron Gallagher." He remembered her speaking those words on the morning they had made love in the shower. She'd prodded and pried, trying to glean bits and pieces of him, but he'd selfishly guarded them, offering only unimportant details of his life. Could he fault her for not trusting when he suffered from the same trait?

He heard her come in from outside, listened as she cleared the table and cleaned up the kitchen. A few minutes later she came through the living room and disappeared up the stairs. Cameron assumed she was on her way to apologize to Rebecca.

The ringing of the phone stirred him from his position and he reached across the sofa to grab the phone on the end table.

"Hello?"

There was a momentary pause. "Cowboy?"

Cameron instantly recognized the deep, bass voice, an unwelcomed reminder of his past. The nickname had started as a joke. Everyone in the bail bond business where Cameron had worked had known he was saving his money for a ranch, saving for the future when he would live the life of a cowboy. The nickname had stuck through his time working as a bounty hunter. "Hi, Jack."

"How are you enjoying the life of a rancher? Bored yet?"

"Not a chance," Cameron returned. His stomach

knotted as he tried to figure out exactly why his old boss had contacted him.

Jack Heggar ran one of the most successful bail bond businesses in the entire state of Montana. He'd never shirked owing much of his success to the team of bounty hunters who worked for him. Samuel and Cameron had been his stars, an unbeatable team when it came to hunting down felons. When Cameron had left Billings and the bounty hunting business behind, he'd assumed he'd never hear from Jack Heggar again.

"Sure miss the good old days when we were all working together." There was another long pause then a whoosh of breath told Cameron Jack had just lit a cigarette.

He could imagine the short, balding man sitting behind his massive oak desk, the surface covered with fast-food wrappers, stained coffee mugs and enough paperwork to belie the rumor of any shortage.

"So what's up, Jack?" Cameron asked, not wanting any foray into the past, when he and Samuel had been partners...friends.

"Apparently you haven't heard the news. I figured living in that one-horse town you probably hadn't heard."

"Heard what?" Cameron asked impatiently.

"He's out, Cameron. Samuel was released from prison late yesterday afternoon."

Cameron's breath caught in his chest as a loud roaring filled his ears. Samuel was out of prison.

Cameron had always known in the back of his mind that eventually Sam would be free.

"Cameron...you there?" Jack's worried voice penetrated through Cameron's shock.

"I'm here." He drew another deep breath. "Okay, so he's out. What does that have to do with me?"

"Rumor has it that he's looking for you. He told his bunk mate he has unfinished business where you're concerned. I figured you had a right to know that he was out. I know there's bad blood between the two of you. Maybe you should keep an eye out over your shoulder."

Cameron frowned and squeezed the bridge of his nose with two fingers. "Sam doesn't know where I live. I left no forwarding address at the Billings apartment. There are only a handful of people who know my current location."

"Yeah...well. Just thought I'd better let you know. You know, Cameron, if the ranching thing doesn't work out, you'll always have a job here with me."

Cameron drew a deep breath. "Thanks, Jack, I appreciate the sentiment, but you know it will never happen. I won't come back...ever. That life is behind me now."

"Too bad. You were one of the best, Cameron. Sometimes you scared me because you were so damned good at ferreting out criminals."

Cameron laughed scathingly. "Oh yeah, I was so good at it I didn't know my own partner was running a scam and breaking all kinds of laws." He cleared his throat, swallowing the lump of bitterness that had lodged there. "Thanks for calling, Jack. I appreciate you keeping me informed."

"If I were you, I'd watch my back." With these ominous words, Jack disconnected.

Cameron hung up, his head reeling with the information Jack had imparted. Unfinished business. As far as Cameron was concerned, there was no such thing between him and Samuel. But apparently Samuel thought otherwise.

He leaned his head back and sighed, remembering Samuel's threats, his words of warning when he'd been arrested. Samuel hadn't believed Cameron would turn him in to the authorities.

Despite Samuel's betrayal, he'd believed Cameron would look the other way or simply walk away. But Cameron had done neither. Still reeling from the shock of finding Samuel and Ginny in bed together, Cameron had gone to his boss and told him of Samuel's criminal activities. Within two days a sting had been arranged and Samuel had been arrested.

And now Samuel had had two long years to allow his anger with Cameron to fester.

Cameron pulled himself up from the sofa, too restless to sit. Going out into the kitchen, he grabbed his coat, jerked it on, then left the house.

He had no destination in mind, just a need to walk and think, to somehow deal with the bitter remnants of the past the phone call had stirred inside him.

He didn't want to face Samuel ever again, didn't

want to remember his love for the man, his love for Ginny and how deeply they both had hurt him.

Samuel would find him. Of that he had no doubt. Sam was an expert at finding people, at following seemingly blank trails, shoving on through dead ends.

Eventually Sam would find him and Cameron would have to face him for the first time since that black day when both their lives had changed forever. If Samuel came with anger and a need for revenge, then Cameron would have to meet him head-on. Cameron would defend himself and all he cared about against Samuel's anger.

Cameron slowed his pace as he came to the stable. Entering it, he went to Sugar's stall. The gentle mare greeted him with a soft whinny, her tail swishing a friendly rhythm. He stood at the stall gate and held out his hand. The horse approached, started to nuzzle him, then backed away with a nervous side step.

She sensed his fear and his despair. Animals were much smarter than people when it came to hidden emotions. Despite his outstretched hand, the horse accurately read the darkness in his heart, the blight on his soul, and she was wary.

He dropped his hand and shoved it into his pocket. Leaning against the side of the stall, he closed his eyes. God, he'd been such a fool to believe he could help Alice, heal the wounding he saw in her eyes. How could he heal her when he couldn't even begin to heal himself?

Alicia stood in the doorway and watched her daughter sleep. There was nothing quite so heart filling as watching a child in slumber. Rebecca sprawled on her back, one foot out of the covers, her lips pursing slightly with each even breath.

How Alicia wished she could give this child of her heart more than an uncertain future. How she wished she could give her stability, a life where they weren't constantly looking over their shoulders.

Alicia had spent the evening with Rebecca, trying to make up for the unpleasantness at dinnertime. Although Rebecca readily forgave her mother for yelling at her, Alicia had a hard time forgiving herself.

Drawing a deep breath, Alicia moved from Rebecca's doorway and into her own bedroom. Her head ached from the tension of the evening and the ten games of Go Fish she'd played with her daughter. Each time Rebecca had won, she'd squealed in a tone that had sent an arrow through Alicia's temples.

She changed into her nightgown, then opened the curtains at the window and peered out into the night. The moon was nearly full, but thick clouds raced across the surface, sporadically obscuring the light that flowed down to the ground.

She'd heard the phone ring earlier, heard the low sounds of Cameron talking, then he'd left the house. That had been hours ago and he had yet to return. She wondered if he'd perhaps gone into town, maybe to the Roundup for a few beers, but his truck was parked out front.

Staring out the window, she thought back to the afternoon. Now, it was hard to believe how she had overreacted to the phone call. Unbelievable that a single call could throw her into such a state of panic.

She started as Cameron came into view, walking from the stables toward the house. He paused, his head tilted upward and she knew he could see her in the window. She suddenly realized that with the light behind her the diaphanous nightgown would appear sheer. She stepped back, quickly turned off the light and got into bed.

Cameron confused her. When he'd come to her while she'd been outside after yelling at Rebecca, he'd displayed a surprising gentleness. Her face burned with the memory of how he had tenderly swept away her tears.

She closed her eyes, her head throbbing at the base of her skull. What she needed was to put this day behind her, hope that she and Rebecca were safe for another day. She needed to sleep, and prayed she wouldn't dream of Cameron. He, too, needed to be put behind her. No matter his gentleness, no matter his kindness, no matter the absolute breathtaking passion he inspired in her, come spring she and Rebecca would move on.

She had no idea how long she'd been asleep when something awakened her. Pulling herself up to a sitting position, she glanced at the clock on the bedside stand. Two o'clock. What had awakened her?

There was usually only one thing that would pull her from her sleep in the middle of the night...one of Rebecca's nightmares. As Alicia got out of bed, she grabbed her robe and pulled it around her. Leaving her darkened bedroom, she was surprised to see a spill of light coming from Rebecca's room and illuminating the hallway.

As she drew near the room, she heard Rebecca's voice, then the deeper, smooth tones of Cameron. She paused just outside the door, leaned against the wall and eavesdropped.

"So, tell me what this dream was about," Cameron said.

"People monsters." Rebecca's reply was a mere whisper, as if she feared saying the words too loudly.

"What's so scary about these people monsters?"

"They want to take me away from my mommy. They tell me my mommy is bad."

Alicia's heart ached as she listened. She hadn't realized before that Rebecca's nightmares were about Broderick and Ruth.

"But you know your mommy isn't bad," Cameron responded.

"I know. But sometimes I'm scared that if the people monsters take me and keep me, I'll forget my mommy." The last words were muffled by a tiny sob.

Alicia started to enter the room, wanting to rock Rebecca in her arms, soothe away her fears. She stopped as she peeked around the corner and saw Cameron holding Rebecca.

"Honey, you know I wouldn't let that happen," Cameron said softly. "I'm a big, strong cowboy and people monsters don't scare me a bit."

"They don't?" Rebecca released her hold from around his neck and peered at him, her eyes wide in astonishment. "How come they don't scare you?"

Cameron smiled and Alicia felt the power of that smile deep inside her. "Because I've got a secret."

Rebecca's eyes shone bright. "A secret? What kind of a secret?"

"I have a magic lariat. Do you know what a lariat is?"

Rebecca nodded proudly. "A rope." She frowned. "Why is it magic?"

"Because no monsters can come inside the circle I draw with it." He stood and mimed holding a rope. "Even though my magic lariat is invisible, its power is awesome and strong. Why don't I throw a lasso around your bed, then no monsters can come and get you while you sleep."

"Yes, please," Rebecca said earnestly.

Alicia watched as Cameron pretended to circle a length of rope over his head. As he "lassoed" the bed, she leaned back against the wall in the hallway.

She'd seen Cameron's passion, had experienced his desire in a beautiful act of lovemaking. But this…this kindness with her daughter, this patience and understanding of people monsters touched her as nothing else.

Maybe it was time she trusted somebody. Maybe that somebody should be Cameron. Perhaps he could see a way out of her troubles. Yes, it was time to tell Cameron from whom she was running and why.

Chapter 9

Alicia had no opportunity to speak to Cameron alone the next morning. Rebecca got up earlier than usual, then couldn't find her homework assignment. As she and her mom scoured their rooms for the missing papers, Cameron left for the day. He wrote her a note, indicating that he was driving into Billings and would be gone all day, but should be home for dinner.

The missing homework assignment was found under Rebecca's bed but by that time she'd missed the bus. Alicia drove her to school, then decided to treat herself to a cup of coffee and a cinnamon roll at the café.

Stella, the waitress who had served them a month before when she and Rebecca had first come to town and stopped at the little café, greeted her with a wide smile. "Hey, nice to see you again. Heard you were working for Cameron Gallagher,'' she said as she poured Alicia a cup of steaming coffee. ''That's one man who is definitely easy on the eyes.'' Stella winked and laughed as Alicia's cheeks warmed. ''Oh, don't tell me you haven't noticed the man is a hunk.''

''I've noticed,'' Alicia admitted with a wry grin.

''I'll be right back with your roll.'' With another hearty chuckle, Stella left Alicia's booth.

Alicia settled back in the booth and sipped her coffee. Several of the patrons smiled and waved to her and she recognized them as people she'd met at the Halloween dance. Good people with moral fiber and a sense of community she'd never felt anywhere else.

She would miss Mustang. If circumstances were different, she and Rebecca could have been happy here for years to come. Again she thought of telling Cameron about their troubles, wondered if perhaps he could help. Oh, it would be heaven to stop running, stop hiding, stop going to sleep each night with fear in her heart.

She smiled as Stella returned holding a saucer with a huge iced cinnamon roll bulging over the edges. ''Just out of the oven,'' she exclaimed.

''It looks positively sinful,'' Alicia replied.

''Enjoy,'' Stella said. ''I've got to get back to the kitchen.''

Alicia enjoyed every bit of the sweet. Her work at the ranch was caught up and with Cameron gone for the day, she decided to linger over a second cup of coffee.

She overheard snatches of conversation around her. Several ranchers at a nearby table bemoaned the coming winter. Two young women talked about a wedding, their voices shrill with excitement as they decided on flowers and colors.

Weddings. Alicia remembered her own, a furtive affair at a justice of the peace. Robert and Alicia both had known his parents didn't approve of Alicia and so they hadn't attempted a traditional church ceremony.

Still, for those brief moments as the justice of the peace had said the words that would make Robert and Alicia husband and wife, Alicia had been filled with happiness.

She hadn't known how difficult the years to come would be, how much her husband was controlled by his cold, autocratic parents. And she hadn't counted on Robert dying and leaving her at the mercy of Broderick and Ruth.

"'Morning Alice. Mind if I join you?''

She looked up to see Jesse Wilder. Clad in his khaki uniform, he looked clean-cut and handsome. Her heart thudded an uneven rhythm that had nothing to do with his attractiveness and everything to do with his job. "Not at all.'' She forced a smile as he slid into the seat across from her.

He signaled Stella for coffee, then smiled at Alicia. "So, what brings you to town this morning? It's rare for you to make an appearance.''

She relaxed slightly. Surely he wouldn't be making small talk if he intended to arrest her. "Rebecca missed the bus this morning so I drove her to school.

I decided to treat myself to one of Stella's cinnamon rolls before heading back to the ranch.''

"Won't be long and the snow will fly, making travel from Gallagher's ranch into town impossible. All the forecasters are calling for a harsh winter.''

"I thought that's the only kind Montana got.''

Jesse laughed, tiny lines wrinkling out from his dark eyes. "Yeah, winter can be pretty rough here. But I imagine you're used to it. Back east they get some pretty good snowstorms.''

She nodded, hoping he didn't pursue this particular topic. Being born and raised in Texas, Alicia had rarely experienced bad winter weather.

Stella appeared at the booth, carrying cup and saucer and a pot of coffee. "If Cameron sees you sitting here flirting with his woman, he'll have your hide,'' she said as she poured the sheriff a cup of the brew.

Jesse laughed and Alicia's cheeks flamed hot. "I'm not Cameron's woman,'' she protested. "I'm his housekeeper.''

Stella grinned and winked. "You can't fool me, Alice. I saw the way the man looked at you at the Halloween dance. And you had that same gleam in your eyes when you looked at him.''

"Don't worry,'' Jesse said. "Stella is just stirring you up. If she had a man of her own she wouldn't have to be so interested in everyone else's love life.''

Stella stuck out her tongue at the handsome sheriff. "You're a heartless man, Jesse Wilder, and that's why no woman will have you.''

Jesse chuckled as Stella flounced away, then turned his gaze back to Alicia. "So, how are you liking our fair little town?"

"It's wonderful. Everyone has been very kind to me."

"It's a town of good people…some better than others, but all of them basically good." Jesse sipped his coffee then set the cup back down. "Makes my job incredibly boring."

"Not much crime?"

Jesse grinned. "One of the waitresses down at the Roundup occasionally gets mad and threatens to shoot a customer, Wes Slader gets drunk once a month and has to be hauled in for disorderly conduct…not exactly violent crimes. Although in the spring when we get an onslaught of wranglers coming to town looking for summer work, I occasionally see more incidents of petty stealing and bar fights."

"But that's one of the things that makes Mustang a terrific place to raise a child," she replied.

He nodded. "And I hope I never have to deal with the kind of crimes officers deal with in bigger cities. Boring is fine with me." He took another gulp of his coffee, then stood. "And speaking of boring…guess it's time for me to get back to work."

"Me, too." Alicia also stood. "Nice seeing you again, Sheriff," she said.

"Jesse," he corrected her.

She smiled. "Nice seeing you again, Jesse."

Within minutes Alicia was back in her car heading toward home. As she drove, her mind skittered from thought to thought, never landing on any one for too long until she thought of Cameron.

A soft smile curved her lips as she remembered how he had thrown the imaginary lasso around Rebecca's bed, promising the magic would keep people monsters at bay. It didn't seem fair that fate had sent her to a man like Cameron, a man whom she could love, if her life wasn't filled with such chaos.

She was nearly to the ranch when the car suddenly went dead. The power steering locked up, the tinny radio stopped playing as the car coasted to a halt.

Grabbing the key, she twisted it and pumped the gas pedal. Nothing. No lights. No power. Nothing. Terrific. She got out of the car and pulled her coat collar closer around her neck. She opened the hood and stared at the dirty engine, the dusty wires, all the pieces and parts she'd never understood.

Helplessly she gazed up the road, then down, hoping for an approaching car. Nothing. No hint of a dust swirl to indicate a vehicle. Sliding back in behind the steering wheel, she tried to find a comfortable position to sit and wait for help.

She hoped she wouldn't have to wait long, although this road wasn't particularly well traveled. If worse came to worse, she supposed she could walk the rest of the way to the ranch. It couldn't be more than two or three miles. She groaned at the very thought.

She'd just about decided to walk when she heard the sound of an approaching pickup. She smiled in relief as the truck pulled up behind her and Trent and Elena got out.

"Got trouble?" Trent asked as he approached.

"Yes. It just quit running. Everything stopped."

"You okay?" Elena asked as she reached Alicia's side.

"Fine," Alicia assured her. "Thankfully it coasted to an easy stop."

Trent disappeared beneath the hood, poking and prodding as if he knew what he was doing. "Good thing we happened along," Elena said.

"I can't tell you how glad I am to see you. I had just decided to walk back to the ranch, and I'm not into long hikes."

Trent reappeared, dusting his hands off with a handkerchief. "Well, it's beyond me. We'll take you home and call Wally at the garage. He can tow it in and figure out what the problem is."

Hopefully fixing the car wouldn't cost too much. Alicia thought of her small cache of money. Expensive car repairs were definitely not in the budget and yet the car was her escape should trouble find them.

Alicia slid into the back of the king cab, next to the car seat that held Trent and Elena's little boy. He slept soundly, one thumb tucked firmly in his rosebud mouth.

Her heart softened as she caught the scent of the baby. She'd once wanted a houseful of children, but she hadn't been able to get pregnant after Rebecca. Now she realized it was a blessing that she hadn't had more children. But there was a part of her heart that still harbored maternal instincts unused.

When they got to Cameron's place, Trent called the garage and arranged for the car to be towed.

"Wally said he'd call you and let you know what the problem is," he said as he hung up the phone. "He'll do right by you. He's a rarity, a good, honest mechanic."

"Thank you so much for bringing me home," Alicia said.

Elena gave her a quick hug. "You've been good for Cameron. He's seemed more at peace lately than I've seen him in a long time." She smiled. "You've become a friend, Alice and I'm very glad you came to Mustang."

Long after Elena and Trent left, Alicia felt the warmth of Elena's words swirling within her heart. Friends…people who cared. She and Rebecca could have that here in Mustang.

She hoped Cameron hurried home. She needed to talk to him. It was time to trust him, and she prayed he'd have some ideas that would make her and Rebecca living in Mustang not just a futile dream…but a reality.

Cameron pulled down the winding driveway that led to his house. The lights burning at the windows of the structure provided a sense of welcome. Although it was just after six, darkness had fallen early and abruptly with a layer of thick clouds obscuring the sky.

For a long moment he sat in the car, staring at the ranch which for the last month had begun to feel more like a home than ever before. And he knew it was because of Rebecca and Alice's presence. Rebecca had filled the house with childish laughter and sunshine smiles, and Alice had brought a new warmth and passion to him.

He raked a hand through his hair, irritated with his meandering thoughts. He was just tired. It had been a hell of a long day. It was nearly a four hour drive to Billings. He'd arrived before noon and had gone to Jack's office, hoping to discover any additional information about Samuel's present whereabouts.

Cameron had hoped to find him, confront him away from the ranch, away from all he held dear. If Samuel was after retribution, then Cameron didn't want him here in Mustang to taint what Cameron had managed to build here.

He'd gone to all their old haunts, the diner where they'd eaten so many meals together, the tavern where they'd hung out to celebrate their many successes. He'd even gone back to his old apartment, and asked the couple living there if anyone had been asking for him. They told him no.

He'd thought Samuel might return to the places he'd been just before his arrest, but nobody had seen him and the trip to Billings proved a waste. He knew he'd learn nothing of substance. But, he'd needed a distraction, any distraction from Alice and the desire he felt for her.

When he'd come out of the stables late the night before, he'd caught sight of her at her bedroom window. Her pale-colored nightgown had appeared translucent with the light shining behind her and he'd wanted to run inside, take her once again and possess her better, more completely than any man ever had...ever would.

That's why he'd run today. Run away from Alice, run away from the feelings and emotions she brought forth from him. With the specter of Sam looming over him he couldn't afford any sort of vulnerability. He had no room for any other emotion except the expectation of Samuel returning to his life seeking revenge.

He got out of the truck and headed into the house, surprised that Alice's car wasn't parked in its usual place. Perhaps she and Rebecca had gone into town for dinner, he thought.

Rebecca greeted him at the door. "Mr. Lallager, we missed you today," she exclaimed. "Mommy made spaghetti for dinner and you missed it."

"I kept a plate warm for you." Alice appeared in the kitchen doorway, a dish towel in hand. She smiled hesitantly.

"Thanks. I thought maybe you two weren't here. Your car is gone." He followed them into the kitchen.

"Mommy's car died," Rebecca informed him as she sat at the table across from him.

Cameron looked at Alice for confirmation. "What happened?"

"According to Wally something with the electrical system quit working. He's ordered some parts so it will be late tomorrow or the day after before the car is fixed." She took an aluminum-foil-covered plate from the oven, removed the foil then set the plate before him.

"Sit down with me." He was suddenly hungry for chatter, anything that might take his mind from Samuel. "Tell me about your day."

Rebecca instantly began to fill him in on everything that had happened that day in school. He learned that Billy Moyer was a bully, Sally Watkins could spit between her teeth and that Brenda Lewis's mom made dumb sandwiches for Brenda's lunch.

As he ate and listened to tidbits from Rebecca's world, the knot in his stomach eased. Thoughts of Samuel Blankenship drifted away beneath the sparkle of the little girl's eyes and the soft, indulgent smiles of her mother.

Once Rebecca had filled him in on the events of her day, she excused herself and went to her room, telling her mom and Cameron that she'd planned a tea party with some of her stuffed animals.

When she was gone, a deep silence fell between Alice and Cameron. As Alice busied herself cleaning up the last of the dishes Cameron watched her. Even with the hair unnaturally dark and her blouse sporting a spaghetti sauce stain, she looked lovely. He felt a familiar stir of desire, a heat he recognized only she evoked in him.

"I'm going to my study," he said as he pushed away from the table, his dinner half-eaten. She looked at him in surprise, but said nothing as he left the kitchen.

In the study Cameron sank into the chair behind his desk. He buried his face in his hands and tried to picture Ginny in his mind. Ginny…the girl he'd believed he loved…the woman he'd planned on marrying. But each time female features came into his head, they somehow transformed into a vision of Alice.

Damn her. Damn Alice, for making him realize he hadn't loved Ginny the way a man should love a woman. Damn Alice for stealing that from him, leaving him more bereft than he'd ever been before.

His love for Ginny had been the one good thing he'd had to hang on to, and now that was gone and there was nothing left, nothing to fill the dark void of despair.

He jumped as a knock fell on the study door. "Yes?"

The door opened and Alice peeked inside. "I'm sorry to bother you, Cameron, but Jesse is here to see you."

"Jesse?" Cameron rose from the desk and followed Alice to the living room, where Jesse stood, hat in hand. He nodded to the sheriff, who smiled tersely. "Something wrong, Jesse?"

"I don't know. Please Alice, stay," he said as she started out of the living room. "I figured I'd better come by here and tell the two of you that some man was in town this afternoon asking a lot of questions about the two of you."

Cameron's guts twisted and adrenaline soared through his veins. He was vaguely aware of Alice's swift intake of breath, the widening of her eyes, but he focused once again on Jesse. "What did he look like?"

"I don't know. Whoever he was, he didn't make his appearance known to me. He spoke to Stella at the café and Mike down at the gas station, wanted to know exactly where your ranch is."

Samuel. It could only be him, Cameron thought. He'd assumed it would take the man a little time to find him. He should have known Samuel was good enough to ferret him out sooner than expected.

"Thanks, Jesse. I appreciate the heads-up."

Jesse shrugged. "I thought it might be something you needed to know." Jesse knew about Cameron's former line of work, apparently had assumed since Cameron's move here that something or someone from that work might come to haunt Cameron.

When Jesse left, Cameron turned to Alice, who'd sank onto the sofa, hands tightly clasped in her lap. "We need to talk," he said.

"About what? There's nothing to talk about." The words came quickly, defensively from her. Her face was pale, her eyes huge.

"I've got something to tell you." He walked across the room and sat down next to her. "You have a right to know what's going on. I think I know who the man was who was in town asking questions."

"Who?" He felt her tension…or was it fear? It rippled from her in waves. Cameron didn't know what caused it, couldn't take the energy to try to figure it out. He knew by telling her about Samuel, he'd only add to whatever burden it was she carried. But she had to know. She had a right to know that she and Rebecca might possibly be in danger.

"His name is Samuel Blankenship. He was released from prison yesterday and I believe he'll be coming for me."

Some of the tension left her and color slowly filtered back into her cheeks. "Who is he and why would he come after you?"

He looked toward the staircase. Rebecca's voice drifted down, barely discernible as she talked to her animals and played a make-believe game. He didn't want Rebecca to hear him, didn't want her to realize that there were real people monsters in the world and no magic lasso he threw could keep them away.

He raked a hand through his hair and chose his words carefully, not wanting to dredge up any more of the past than was necessary. "Samuel and I were partners. We worked together for several years. Samuel began breaking the law, taking payoffs instead of doing his job. I was instrumental in getting him arrested and sent to prison. I think he's coming after me looking for revenge."

"You were more than partners, weren't you?"

He looked at her, surprised by her perceptive guess. "Yeah…we were best friends…like brothers. I thought I knew his heart better than anyone. I trusted him like I never trusted anyone in my life…and he betrayed that trust." His final words rang with bitterness.

Again his stomach knotted painfully and he stood, unable to sit next to her and speak of Ginny. He didn't want to talk about Ginny at all, but the emotions he'd tapped pressed hard and tight in his chest, and he had to release them. "There was a woman.

Her name was Ginny. She was twenty-one when I met her. She was working as a checker in a supermarket. Her parents were dead and she was alone in the world, struggling to get by and trying to save money for college.''

He paced the length of the room, then back again, remembering Ginny as she had been in those early days of their friendship. She'd been a sweet girl, eager to please and hungry for approval. ''I loved her. She reminded me of Elena in a lot of ways. We talked about the future, planned our lives together. Eventually we moved in together.''

Leaning against the fireplace, he stared at a spot just over Alice's left shoulder, unable to meet her gaze as his memories swept over him. ''The three of us, Ginny, Samuel and I were together all the time. I was working a part-time security job as well as my work with Samuel, and sometimes when I had to work, I encouraged Samuel to take Ginny to the movies or out to eat so she wouldn't get lonely without me.'' He laughed, a bitter expulsion of energy.

He turned to face the fireplace. ''Surely you can guess the rest. It's such a damned cliché. I came home from work early one day and caught the two of them in bed together.''

He jumped as Alice's hand touched his arm. He turned to see her eyes filled with tears…the tears he had never cried, the tears he couldn't cry. ''Oh Cameron, I'm so sorry. You must have been so hurt…felt so betrayed.''

He stepped away from her, fighting the impulse to clutch her in his arms, lose his memories and himself in her sweet warmth. He'd told her she couldn't hide in him, and he refused to hide in her.

"Anyway...that day I stood in the bedroom long enough to tell Samuel he was a dead man, then I left. I walked for hours, trying to get rid of the most enormous rage I'd ever felt. When I finally returned to the apartment Ginny and all her things were gone."

"You never saw or heard from her again?" Alice asked softly.

He shook his head. "Anyway, I got word that Samuel told his bunk mate in prison that he had unfinished business with me. I'm sure he hates me for being responsible for sending him to prison."

"You said you and this man worked together. What kind of work did you do?" Alice asked.

He hesitated before answering, oddly for the first time in his life not proud of what he'd done before. "Bounty hunting."

Once again the color seeped from her cheeks. "Bounty hunting?" She repeated the words as if they were foreign to her.

"Yeah, you know, we hunted fugitives from justice and made sure they faced their day in court."

"Mommy, I gave my teddy a bath and now he's all icky." Rebecca's distressed voice drifted down the stairs.

"I'd better go up to her," Alice said, her voice high and strained. She turned and raced up the stairs. Cameron stared after her, wondering what the hell he had said that had her looking like a stunned deer in the glare of headlights.

Chapter 10

A bounty hunter. Dear God in Heaven, she'd chosen a bounty hunter's house in which to hide. A bounty hunter...a man who hunted criminals for a living, a man who detained and arrested people for money.

She and Rebecca had to leave...they had to run, from this house, from this man before he found out that she was probably a fugitive from justice.

She paced the confines of her bedroom, her mind whirling. After learning his previous occupation, she'd somehow managed to pass the remainder of the evening as if nothing was wrong, as if her nerves weren't jumping, her adrenaline not pumping. She'd dried Teddy, bathed and tucked Rebecca into bed, then had come to her bedroom to think...and plan.

Thank God. She moved to the window and stared out into the dark of night. Thank God she hadn't told Cameron anything about her past…about Broderick and Ruth's threats.

Alicia had read enough about bounty hunters, seen enough movies about them that she knew most of them would turn in their own mother if the bounty price was big enough.

It was obvious from the condition of the ranch that Cameron wasn't exactly prosperous. How much money would Broderick have placed on her head? Most assuredly a small fortune.

Would her night of lovemaking with Cameron circumvent any desire Cameron had in turning her in? It was a chance she didn't want to take.

They had to leave. She moved to the window and frowned into the dark, moonless sky. They couldn't leave tonight. She had no car. An hysterical burst of laughter threatened to escape her lips.

How ironic, that the ranch where she'd chosen to hide was owned by a bounty hunter. Did life get more incongruous than this?

She left the window and paced the floor of the bedroom. Okay, they couldn't leave tonight, but Wally said he hoped to have her car ready sometime late tomorrow.

In the morning when Cameron was outside, she would pack them up. When Wally called to say her car was ready, she'd have Cameron take her to the garage, she'd drive back here and pretend nothing was the matter.

Then, tomorrow night while he slept, she and Rebecca would leave…disappear from his life. She sank down onto the edge of her bed, her heart aching as she thought of never seeing Cameron again.

She was precariously close to falling in love with him, had been perilously close to telling him her secrets…secrets that could have yielded him enough money to build an empire, secrets that would have Alicia losing the most precious thing in her life…Rebecca.

She sighed and bit back hot tears. Rebecca. She'd blossomed in their time here, blossomed beneath Cameron's gentle care. She would be crushed when Alicia told her they had to leave, that it was once again time to pack up and start anew someplace else.

Rebecca had begun to think of the Last Hope Ranch as home. Her nightmares came less frequently and her smile and laughter more readily. She'd felt safe here, secure in the knowledge that Cameron the cowboy would keep her safe.

"Dammit." Alicia swiped at her tears and curled up on the bed. She was tired. So very tired. Exhausted from worry, from looking over her shoulder, tired of being afraid every minute of every day. When would it end? Would it ever end? With a weary sigh, she gave into the sleep that beckoned, knowing that when she awakened it would once again be time to run.

She awoke just after dawn and pulled herself hurriedly out of bed. She'd forgotten to set the alarm the night before and was later than usual.

As she dressed, she smiled bitterly at her thoughts. So, she was late? What was Cameron going to do…fire her? She wasn't staying anyway.

Still, aware that she needed to keep things as normal as possible, once dressed she hurried to the kitchen, surprised to find Cameron there and the coffee already made.

"I'm sorry I'm late. I overslept."

He shrugged. "Doesn't matter this morning. Not much work will get done today."

She looked at him in surprise. "Why?"

He gestured toward the window. "Haven't you looked outside?"

Dread building inside her, she approached the window and peered out. Snow. Mounds of it. It already completely covered the ground and continued to fall from the sky in copious thick flakes.

Alicia stifled a low moan. She whirled around to face Cameron. "Have you heard the weather forecast?"

"Yeah. They're calling for snow," he said dryly.

"How much?"

"A foot has already fallen and there's no end in sight. I'd say you are getting your first taste of Montana winter in a big gulp."

She wanted to scream. She wanted to cry. She wanted him to hold her and tell her everything would be all right. Instead she poured herself a cup of coffee and tried to pretend the snow didn't devastate her, her life wasn't overwhelming her.

When Jesse had first shown up the night before and told them about somebody asking questions, her initial thought had been that Broderick had found them. It was only after Cameron had told her about

Samuel Blankenship that her nerves had calmed down.

She hoped he was right. She hoped it was Samuel looking for Cameron and not Broderick seeking her. She'd tried to be so careful, tried so desperately hard not to do anything that would leave a trail, point a finger to their whereabouts.

She sipped her coffee and sat down at the table across from Cameron. The heat of the coffee found the cold places inside her with soothing warmth. Okay, it was snowing. Surely in the next day or so her car would be fixed and the roads would be cleared. As she relaxed, Cameron's words from the night before replayed in her mind.

Last night when he'd told her about Samuel and Ginny, she'd been too distraught about her own problems to consider his. Now the import of his words slammed into her.

According to Cameron this man, this Samuel Blankenship was coming after him with anger and a need for revenge burning in his heart. Was it possible Samuel Blankenship meant to kill Cameron?

How could Cameron sit so calmly, sipping his coffee as if he hadn't a care in the world? How could he speak of revenge and retribution as if it were a natural part of his world? What kind of a man was he?

''Are you frightened?'' The words left her mouth before she was conscious of them forming in her head.

''Frightened? Of the snow?'' One dark eyebrow quirked upward.

"No...of this Samuel. Aren't you afraid of confronting him?"

His features tightened and a muscle throbbed in the side of his neck. For a long moment he stared into his coffee cup, the throb of the muscle increasing with each breath he took. "I don't go looking for trouble, but if it finds me I'll deal with it. I guess I'll just have to deal with Samuel when he appears."

"I'm not sure I understand. If you were bounty hunters working together, how was he cheating and betraying you?"

Cameron waited before answering. He finished the coffee in his cup, then stood and poured himself another. He rubbed a hand across his brow, as if the very act of thinking back to that time in his life made him weary.

He didn't answer until he was once again seated across from her. "I don't even know when his deceptions began. We'd been close as brothers, partners for three years when I noticed our success rate had dropped dramatically. We'd get tips about a criminal's whereabouts, but it seemed when we got to that particular place, we were too late and he'd already moved on. There were times we missed them by mere hours. Once or twice, I wouldn't have suspected anything, but it was happening again and again."

"Samuel was warning them?"

He nodded, his eyes dark and hooded. "I didn't want to believe it at first." He rubbed his forehead, then raked his hand down and across his jaw. "I suspected, but I couldn't believe, didn't want to believe.''

He sighed and leaned back in the chair. ''He was finding them and giving them an opportunity to pay him rather than be hauled in. They'd pay him off and he'd give them twenty-four hours to disappear.''

''What happened? When you finally figured out what he was doing, what did you do?''

Again a look of intense weariness swept over his features, making her sorry she'd asked, sorry she'd dug into areas of such apparent pain.

''For a while, I did nothing. I kept thinking Samuel would stop, would turn around, would realize what a mistake he was making. But, when he didn't stop, I had to make a decision. It was the most difficult decision I've ever made. I had to turn him in.''

His features tightened, the weariness falling away. ''He made a mockery of everything we stood for, he traded money for his honor and assumed I'd cover for him.'' His eyes glittered dangerously. ''I misjudged him, but he definitely misjudged me.''

Alice realized now why Cameron was a man who kept to himself, refused to allow anyone close to him. Betrayed by the woman he loved and by his best friend, it was no wonder he was afraid to trust anyone.

And she was no better than Samuel and Ginny. She'd betrayed Cameron as well, lying to him about her past, about her present. He didn't even know her real name.

Remorse swept through her, a deep ache for herself…a mirror ache for him. She longed to confess to him, but fear had become such an integral part of her life and she simply couldn't overcome it to make a confession to him.

She poured herself another cup of coffee and sank down at the table. "When do you expect this Samuel to show up?" She suddenly realized if danger approached Cameron, it also came far too close to her and Rebecca.

"The snow bought me some time. Samuel hates snow." He laughed, a short, staccato burst that had nothing to do with merriment. "He's almost phobic in his hatred of snow. He'll hole up someplace until the storm is over."

"And when the storm is over?"

He raked a hand through his hair and expelled a deep sigh. "Then he'll come."

She fought the impulse to reach out to him. "I'm frightened for you." He looked at her in surprise. "You should have told Jesse," she continued. "You should have insisted he put a guard on you or something."

Cameron smiled, although the gesture did little to lighten the darkness in his eyes. "Somehow I feel like this confrontation with Samuel has to happen." His hand tightened around his coffee mug, so tight his knuckles whitened. "We need closure between us."

"But you said yourself he's coming for revenge, not closure. He could kill you." She finally said the words that sent horror sweeping through her.

"I intend to do my best to see that doesn't happen," he replied dryly. "My concern is for you. I thought about this all night long, about you and Rebecca and Samuel. The man I knew would never do anything to hurt a woman or a child, but I don't know how much prison time has changed Samuel.''

It was a perfect opening, a perfect way for her to leave and not have Cameron suspect her reasons for leaving. She got up and moved to the window. The snow still fell, the wind creating drifts in the snow that had already fallen.

Time. The snowstorm bought her a little more time with Cameron. When the snow stopped and the roads cleared, Samuel would come for Cameron and Alicia would leave with Rebecca.

She turned back to Cameron. ''If Rebecca and I leave here…you could come with us. We could travel for a while or find someplace to stay until Samuel gets tired of looking for you. Surely he won't hunt for you forever. Eventually he'll want to get on with his life.''

His gaze held hers, sharp and focused. ''I'm not willing to run from what chases me. I won't spend the rest of my life looking over my shoulder.''

''Mommy…snow! It's snowing!'' Rebecca's excited squeals preceded her into the kitchen, halting the conversation between the two adults. ''Can we go out and play in it? I want to play in it and build a snowman with a carrot nose and a gumdrop smile. Please…please…I got my fingers crossed.''

''First things first,'' Alicia told her daughter. ''And first is breakfast.''

As she began making the morning meal, despair swept through her. She loved Cameron. She could no longer fool herself, no longer deny the emotion that filled her heart, beat in her veins.

She loved him with all her heart, all her soul. She had no idea what he felt for her, and in any case it didn't matter. As long as he refused to run and she refused to stop running, it simply didn't matter.

Cameron stood at the window, sipping coffee and watching Rebecca and Alice frolic in the snow. It had snowed hard nearly all day and Alice had insisted Rebecca wait to play outside until it eased up a little. She'd managed to put Rebecca off until after they'd eaten an early supper. By then the flurry of heavy snow had ebbed and gigantic fluffy flakes floated down from the heavy gray clouds.

The two females were busy rolling balls to form a snowman. The base had already been done and they now worked to roll the middle section.

A grudging smile curved his lips as Alice lost her footing and fell. Her laughter mingled with Rebecca's and rang through the pane of glass to him. They appeared to be having such fun.

Fun. Cameron had never built a snowman, and he couldn't remember the last time he'd had fun. It had definitely been a long time before Alice and Rebecca had moved in with him.

Over the weeks there had been moments in their daily routine when laughter had prevailed and a sense of fun had coursed through him. Fun and memories, that's what Rebecca and Alice had brought to him. The memory of their days in his home were pleasant ones, untainted by ugliness like his other memories.

Before he could change his mind, he raced up the stairs, grabbed a few items, then pulled on an extra pair of socks and an insulated shirt and his heavy winter jacket.

"Hey Mommy, look! Mr. Lallager's come to play," Rebecca exclaimed as Cameron approached them.

Alice's cheeks were a bright pink, flushed from the cold and her exertions. Her eyes sparkled with merriment as she saw what Cameron carried. "I think he's come to help us make our snowman into a cowboy snowman."

"Oh boy!" Rebecca shouted with glee. "A cowboy snowman!"

"First we need to finish the snowman," Cameron said. He set down the items he had brought from his closet, then moved to help Alice lift the middle section of the snow creature onto the awaiting base.

Within minutes the snowman was complete and to Rebecca's delight, Cameron placed an old western hat atop the snowman's head, a kerchief around his neck and a huge golden belt buckle in the center of his "belly." Two tin can lids gave him wide, silver eyes and red gumdrops provided a wide, happy smile. Rebecca giggled at the end result.

"And now you know what I think it's time for?" Cameron looked at Rebecca, then at Alice.

"What?" Rebecca asked as she jumped up and down and clapped her hands together.

"A snowball fight!" He grabbed a handful of

snow and threw it at the little girl. Rebecca squealed as Alice armed herself with quickly made snowballs.

A flurry of snowballs filled the air along with cries of success, howls of defeat and laughter. Cameron was faster at making and flinging snowballs, but Alice had an unerring aim and more than once he was caught midchest by a well-thrown ball.

Several times Cameron stood still so one of Rebecca's balls could catch him, simply because he loved the sound of her merriment when she managed to hit him.

By the time the fight was over, they were all wet, cold and more than ready to go inside. The skies had once again opened, the snowfall heavy enough to cut visibility.

"How about I build a big fire," Cameron said as they entered through the back door.

"And I'll make us some hot chocolate," Alice said, both she and Cameron earning a smile of approval from Rebecca.

After changing clothes, Cameron built a roaring fire in the fireplace. Drifting down from the upstairs were Rebecca and Alice's voices as they changed out of their sodden clothing.

He leaned back on his haunches and watched the dancing flames of the fire. It had been fun…playing in the snow, laughing together and acting like a family.

A family. He hadn't thought of having his own for a long time. He and Ginny had made plans, but when she had left, she'd taken all his dreams with her.

He sat all the way down and held his hands out toward the fire. The female voices drifting down the stairs were sweetly melodic, pleasantly familiar and he closed his eyes and allowed the noise to soothe over him, like cooling balm against a burning wound.

With the heat of the fire warming the front of him, his thoughts turned to Alice. Alice, with her sweet scent and smiling eyes. Alice, with those luscious lips that always looked as if they ached to be kissed.

He'd love to have her here right now, beneath him in front of the fireplace. It was far too easy to imagine how the glow of the fire would paint her skin in soft gold tones, how her eyes would glow like the dancing flames when he stroked down the length of her.

He sighed. Foolish thoughts. It would be utterly foolish to make love with her, to once again enjoy the sweet release of possessing her completely.

When it stopped snowing, he knew she would leave. He wanted her to leave. He couldn't take a chance on her and Rebecca's well-being. He didn't know what to expect from Samuel, but wanted to take no chances where Alice and Rebecca were concerned.

He opened his eyes as Alice came down the stairs, the scent of her perfume preceding her. "Hmm, you look warm and comfortable."

He smiled. "I am."

"Hot chocolate will just take a few minutes." With those words she disappeared into the kitchen.

Light footsteps sounded on the stairs as Rebecca

ran toward him. Clad in a light pink fleece pajama top and pants, she looked snugly warm. "Oh, a fire," she exclaimed and sat down next to Cameron.

She leaned into him, as if it were the most natural thing in the world to do. Cameron's heart spasmed unexpectedly.

Children weren't afraid to give their hearts, to expose their feelings openly and freely. It hadn't occurred to Rebecca that Cameron might rebuff her. She liked him and with a child's presumption knew he liked her, too.

Cameron once again stared at the fire, wishing things were that uncomplicated for him. He remembered the conversation he'd had with Alice, when he'd tried to convince her that pain made you stronger, and she'd insisted that pain made you afraid.

He realized now she was right. He'd been afraid…was afraid to trust in his own feelings, afraid to give any piece of his heart to another. Ginny and Samuel and their betrayal had destroyed his capacity to love anyone else.

Rebecca's weight against his side suddenly felt unusually heavy. He looked down to see that she had fallen sound asleep. The play outside in the snow had worn her out.

He leaned down and pressed his mouth against her forehead, wishing he could be different for her, wishing he wasn't so damned afraid. She smiled in her sleep, as if in some part of her sleeping mind she registered the soft kiss with pleasure.

"Here we are…three steaming cups of hot chocolate complete with tons of marshmallows." Alice set the tray she carried down on the coffee table, then smiled at Cameron and her slumbering daughter. "Too much snow play."

"Apparently," he agreed.

"I'll just carry her up to bed." She bent down to lift the little girl.

Cameron stood and scooped Rebecca up in his arms. "She's too heavy for you. I'll take her."

He followed her up the stairs, trying to ignore the sexy sway of her hips that seemed to taunt him. When they got to Rebecca's room, he gently placed the sleeping child on the bed.

Her eyes fluttered open and she smiled. "I had the bestest day," she said, her voice slow and heavy with sleep.

"I'm glad," he said, unable to remain untouched by the absolute sweetness of her.

"Go back to sleep, sweetheart," Alice said as she tucked Rebecca in beneath the blankets.

"Will there still be snow tomorrow?" she asked.

Alice laughed and Cameron smiled. "Yes, honey. The snow will still be there when you wake up," Alice answered.

"Can we all play again? Like today?" The question was directed at Cameron, as if Rebecca knew her mother would play with her, and hoped that Cameron would, too.

"I think I can arrange another awesome snowball fight," Cameron replied.

"I hope we always stay here with Mr. Lallagher. I like us all together." Rebecca closed her eyes, her words slurring together. "I got my fingers dou-ble…double crossed." Her breathing once again be-came deep and regular, signaling a fall back into the arms of slumber.

As Alice kissed her daughter's forehead, Cameron left the room, his heart in turmoil as Rebecca's sleepy words echoed in each chamber.

The little girl was obviously hungry for a father figure, wanted the security of a family. But Cameron wasn't the right man to make that particular dream of hers come true. He'd died emotionally two years before, and dead men didn't make good father fig-ures.

"I'll bet she'll sleep the whole night through," Alice said as she joined Cameron in front of the fire. "She was exhausted." She handed Cameron a cup of the hot chocolate, then sat down next to him.

He sipped the sweet hot drink and watched her as she stared pensively into the fire. Her lashes cast long shadows on her cheeks and the firelight brushed her dark hair with red-gold highlights. She looked lovely and somehow sad.

"Even if Samuel wasn't coming here, even if there was no danger whatsoever, you'd be leaving soon, wouldn't you?"

She turned, her eyes registering surprise at his question. For a moment he thought she might con-tinue her story, tell him one more lie. Instead she sighed, raked a hand through her hair and nodded.

"And you aren't really from Pennsylvania."

"Please, don't ask me anything else, Cameron. I

don't want to tell any more lies, and I can't risk telling you the truth.''

Frustration tore at him. ''Why not?'' He set his mug aside and scooted closer to her. ''What could be so terrible that you couldn't tell me?''

She chewed her bottom lip, her expression troubled. ''It isn't anything horrible or terrible. I haven't murdered anyone or stolen anything.'' She caught her bottom lip between her teeth once again. ''Please…just leave it alone.''

''Are you running from your husband?''

''No. Robert's death wasn't a lie.'' She pulled her legs up against her chest and wrapped her arms around them, once again staring into the fire. ''Everything I told you about my marriage to Robert was true…how we met…how he died.'' She shook her head slightly. ''Let's talk about something else. How's Mischief doing since you moved her inside?''

Cameron's frustration mounted, but he tamped it down, realizing nothing he could say, nothing he could do would make her tell him what he wanted to know.

He frowned as he thought of the wild mare. ''I can't get her to trust me at all. Physically, she's doing all right, but mentally I'm a little worried about her. The spirit she exhibited for so long seems to be gone.''

''But I thought that was what you wanted. I thought you wanted to break her.''

''I wanted her to trust me…I didn't want to steal her spirit.''

"So what are you going to do?"

He picked up his mug and took a sip, then placed it back on the floor beside him. "I'm not sure." He stared at Alice meaningfully. "I guess I keep working with her, hope she eventually learns to trust me, that I won't hurt her."

For a long moment their gazes remained connected and to his surprise hers filled with tears and a small sob escaped from her. Instantly he pulled her into his arms. "I'm sorry. I didn't mean to push you too hard."

His words only seemed to make things worse as her tears came faster and she sobbed again. He stroked her back, damning himself for pressing the issue. He'd learned with the horse that it was impossible to bend somebody's will through sheer force. Besides, he wanted her to come to him, wanted her to trust him, confide in him willingly.

"What can I do, Alice?" he asked softly as he continued to hold her close. "Tell me what I can do to help."

She raised her head and looked at him, her eyes still filled with glittering tears. "Make it snow forever," she answered, and he tightened his arms around her, wishing he could do just that.

Chapter 11

Alicia didn't know who made the first move. One moment she was crying in his arms, the next moment they were kissing...a kiss of infinite tenderness.

Cameron's hands cupped either side of her face as his lips plied hers with sweet heat. Alicia melted against him, into him, wishing it would snow forever, keep them together until they were old and gray and Rebecca was an adult with a family of her own.

She tasted her tears mingling with the flavor of hot chocolate and Cameron. His tongue swirled with hers, creating shivers of pleasure that raced up and down her spine.

She was cold...and he warmed her. She was frightened...and he soothed her. Everything she wanted was inside him. Everything she needed, he had.

"Alice. Sweet Alice," he whispered against her neck, and in that instant Alicia knew she had to tell him.

She was so tired of living a lie, of answering to a name other than her own. She had to take a chance. She loved him enough to trust him.

She gently pushed out of his arms and scooted away from him. Staring at the fire, she felt his puzzled gaze on her. "My name isn't Alice Burwell. It's Alicia Randall." She turned her head and looked at him. He nodded, apparently encouraging her to go on.

"My husband wasn't an orphan. I didn't meet his parents until after we were married. They hated me from the very beginning." She looked back at the fire, remembering the first time she'd met Broderick and Ruth.

She'd been young and naive, and believed herself madly in love with Robert. "They were cruel and hateful not only to me but to Robert. They told him it wasn't necessary for him to marry the first common piece he'd slept with, that they would pay for an annulment and give me money to go away."

She drew a deep breath and gazed at Cameron once again. "Robert told them both to go to hell, that we were married and we intended to stay married. It was the first and only time he ever stood up to them."

She stood, unable to sit and dredge up the past, the memories that formed a knot in the pit of her stomach. She had been so stupid, so innocent, and so desperate for family.

She'd wanted Broderick and Ruth to accept her, to love her and she and Robert had tried so hard to make that happen.

"What does all this have to do with your running?" Cameron asked.

"In order to understand what's happened, you have to understand Robert's relationship with his parents. They were intrinsically tied together. Robert worked for the family business, his parents owned the house where he lived, he was given an allowance to live on rather than a salary."

She clutched her hands together before her, the memories sweeping over her. "They controlled everything we did, where we went, who we socialized with…everything. I was in my own little world, preparing for Rebecca's birth. It wasn't until Rebecca was about a year old that I realized how controlled we were by Broderick and Ruth."

She paused and walked over to the window. Peering out she saw the snow was still falling. They were still safe…at least for the moment. Cameron got up from in front of the fire and sat down on the sofa. He gestured for her to join him there, but she shook her head, needing to pace while she confronted her past.

"Robert grew more and more unhappy each day, but he didn't know how to break away from them. He didn't have the emotional strength to make the break…and then he died."

"And left you all alone to cope with his parents."

Tears blurred her vision as she looked at Cameron and nodded her head. "Right after his death, I tried...I really tried to be there for Broderick and Ruth. No matter what kind of people I believed they were, they had lost their only son and I thought in our shared grief we might find some peace. And for a while, that's what I believed was happening. They were kind to me and Rebecca, and in my own grief I desperately wanted them to be my family, too."

Again tears burned hot in her eyes as she remembered those days immediately following Robert's death. She had plunged into a dark despair unlike any she'd ever known. She was alone with Rebecca...and frightened, their future uncertain as she realized everything she had belonged to Broderick and Ruth.

Mourning Robert's death, guilty with the knowledge that she'd never loved him like she should have, when his parents had asked if Rebecca could spend an occasional night with them, she agreed, wanting to be a good daughter-in-law, wanting to encourage Rebecca's relationship with her grandparents.

"Alicia." Cameron's hands on her shoulders pulled her from the past. His eyes were gentle as he used a finger to swipe at her tears. "Are you okay?"

She nodded and leaned against him, burrowing her face in the front of his shirt. "After Robert's death, his parents took more interest in Rebecca." It was easier to go back to the past with his arms wrapped around her and his heart beating next to hers. "Once a week or so she'd spend the night with them and then they'd bring her home late the next day. I wanted her to have a relationship with them, wanted her to have a sense of family that I never had. Then about four months ago they came to me and offered to pay me fifty thousand dollars to disappear."

She felt Cameron's swift intake of breath and she looked up at him once again. "They wanted Rebecca."

"They are the people monsters Rebecca dreams about," he said.

"Yes. Although it wasn't until recently that I made the connection. Of course I told Broderick and Ruth to keep their money, that I didn't intend to go anywhere without my daughter. And that's when Broderick told me he'd already started the paperwork to have me declared an unfit mother and custody of Rebecca granted to them. That night Rebecca and I ran."

"But Alicia, you aren't an unfit mother," Cameron said, a thumb caressing the side of her face. "I've seen you with your daughter, watched you in your daily interaction with her. You're a good mother."

"You don't understand," she exclaimed, frustration rising inside her. She stepped out of his embrace and wrapped her arms around her shoulders, chilled to the bone with thoughts of losing Rebecca.

"They have money, Cameron. Enough money to pay witnesses, buy doctor reports. They can make me be whatever they want me to be…a drunk, a junkie, an abusive or neglectful mother. You don't know these people, Cameron. They aren't going to let a little thing like the truth keep them from what they want…and they want my daughter." Her voice rose, almost hysterical by the time she finished.

"So, you've been running."

She nodded and swallowed hard to control her emotions. "I'm sure Broderick has hired investigators to hunt for me so we've been moving around a lot, never staying in one place for more than a night or two. When I left, I didn't have access to very much money. A couple thousand dollars. The rest is tied up with the business and in trust funds. I finally ran out of money when we landed here in Mustang. My plan was to work until I got together enough money to mount some sort of a legal defense."

He smiled mirthlessly. "On the salary I'm paying you that would have taken quite a while."

"But it was a start, and Rebecca has been so happy here. Each day I thought of moving on, but I couldn't. For just a little while I wanted us to be normal, to live like normal people and actually have a life."

"And eventually you would have left." His voice was strangely flat.

"Yes." The admission escaped her softly, like a mournful sigh. "Unless somebody spooked me, I'd intended to stay until spring. But it looks like your Samuel is bringing spring a little early this year."

He shoved his hands in his pockets. "Why didn't you tell me all this before?"

Her cheeks warmed. "I was afraid. I know Broderick has probably offered a sizable reward for information about my whereabouts.'' She looked around the room. ''You aren't exactly living in the lap of luxury here.''

A muscle in his jaw ticked ominously. ''And so you assumed I could be bought?''

She sighed, recognizing his rising anger. ''Cameron, I've lived the last several months of my life so afraid. Trust isn't something that has come easily to me. I'm telling you this now because I know the man you are, I believe in your character.''

''So what are your plans? To keep running? Keep looking over your shoulders? Keep dragging Rebecca from place to place, school to school?''

Defensive anger rose inside her. ''I don't have any other alternative.''

''Sometimes you have to face your monsters, Alicia. It's the only way to be rid of them.''

''I can't,'' she whispered with despair. ''I just can't risk it. The price of losing Rebecca is too high for any sort of a gamble.''

He studied her face, his gaze steady as if memorizing it forever. ''Then you'll have no life, no future, nothing for yourself.''

Alicia's heart constricted painfully. She'd already faced that reality…the pain of loving Cameron and knowing nothing could ever come of it. ''That's the price I pay to keep my daughter safe.''

''It's one hell of a high price.''

''She's worth it.''

He nodded his agreement.

There seemed to be nothing left to say between them. Alicia sank down on the sofa, depleted from the emotional turmoil of dredging up her past, aching with the fact that no matter how deeply, how completely she loved this man, there was no future for her here…or anywhere.

Cameron joined her on the sofa, sitting close enough to her that their thighs touched. ''Surely this Broderick and Ruth have skeletons in their closets, something you could use as leverage against them.'' His hand absently played with a strand of her hair.

''If they have skeletons, they're buried deep.'' She closed her eyes, trying to remove herself from the sweetness of his touch.

''Maybe you just haven't dug deeply enough.''

Alicia frowned, a nebulous thought working to become clear. Something niggled at her brain…a distant memory, an unfinished thought…but it refused to surface fully formed. And in any case, Cameron's touch on her hair, his thumb rubbing along the side of her face made any serious thought difficult.

She leaned her head over to his shoulder, her hand falling on his thigh. She felt his muscles tense beneath her palm and her heart quickened in response.

It was crazy to want him now…with the knowledge that she would probably be leaving within the next twenty-four to forty-eight hours. And yet when she looked into his eyes, she saw the same craziness shining there.

She moaned with what she thought was protest, but as his lips claimed hers she realized it hadn't been a protest at all, but rather an agreement to the unspoken question in his eyes.

She opened her mouth to his, eagerly encouraging him to claim her with fire, brand her with flames of possession. She wanted him to make love to her one last time…a final memory she could carry in her heart as she moved from place to place, from town to town.

Cameron clutched her to him, as if he, too, needed one last chance to hold her, caress her. His lips left hers, blazing a trail along her jawline, burning their way down her throat.

She dropped her head back, her hands tangling in his hair as his mouth pressed against the hollow of her throat. Tears begged to be released…tears of immense joy mingling with tears of aching sorrow.

Her love for Cameron filled her heart. He was all she'd ever dreamed of, both for herself and for Rebecca. She wanted to tell him, wanted him to know that she hadn't believed in passion and love-ever-after until him…but the words refused to come. What was the point?

It was enough for her to know of the love that burned within her heart. It wasn't necessary for him to know, especially when if he wanted more, she couldn't give him more. She couldn't give him anything but tonight.

As his hands slid up her back, his fingers deftly unfastened her bra. "Not here," she said, knowing it was possible Rebecca could awaken and stumble downstairs. "In my room. In my bed."

He nodded and stood, then held out his hand to her. Together they walked up the stairs, their hands linked as if they were one. When they reached her bedroom, he undressed her, then hurriedly took off his own clothes.

The room was chilly and they slid beneath the blankets, their bodies instantly finding each other and sharing body heat. Alicia reveled in the feel of his naked body against hers, the tactile pleasure of his hairy chest against her bare breasts, his strong, masculine legs rubbing along her sleek, slender ones.

She pressed against him, her body conforming to the contours and planes of his. They fit together like interlocking puzzle pieces, no gaps, no space...a perfect fit.

His hands cupped her breasts, fingers teasing the taut nipples. She could feel the calluses on his palms, a remainder of his present life as a hard-working rancher.

Her fear when she'd learned he was a bounty hunter now seemed distant and unreal. She should have known that Cameron wouldn't betray her, that if nothing else, his love for Rebecca would prevail against any lure of money.

She moaned as his tongue found a swollen nipple. He teased with his tongue and teeth and she splayed her hands in his hair, loving the feel of the silky strands tangling around her fingers.

As his mouth found hers once again, she tasted desperation, knew it was her own. Unless it snowed forever, tonight would probably be the last time she would feel Cameron's body against hers and taste the heat of his mouth. Tonight would be the last time she'd feel his hands caressing her skin, the last time he'd possess her body and soul.

When he finally entered her, she released a cry of joy and anguish. The joy of his possession was tempered by the agony of knowing that like the color of her hair, and the comfort of her previous life, Cameron would be one more sacrifice she'd have to bear.

Cameron stood at the bedroom window and stared out into the winter wonderland. It had stopped snowing and the clouds had parted to expose the moon.

The lunar light sparkled on the crusty snow, creating a postcard-perfect picture, but Cameron found no beauty in the stillness of the night.

He wished for raging winds and blowing snow, for blizzard conditions and roads slick with ice. He raked a hand through his hair and sighed, confused with his thoughts, bewildered by his emotions.

He turned from the window and looked at the woman sleeping on the bed. In the pale moonlight that seeped through the window, her sleeping features were painted in a silvery light. Her dark hair spilled onto the pristine pillow beneath her. Her lips were reddened, still slightly swollen from their kissing. She looked positively beautiful.

He cared about her…deeply, but it wasn't love. It couldn't be love because he'd promised himself he'd never, ever love again.

Once again he slid a hand through his hair, wondering how long it would be before the roads were cleared. How long before snowplows made paths for easy traveling? How long before Alicia and Rebecca left him?

Pain shot through him as he thought of being alone once again...of eating meals without Rebecca's chatter, of not seeing Alicia's smile each and every day.

He leaned his forehead against the window, the glass frigid against his skin. He'd miss them. He would miss Rebecca, and God, how he would miss Alicia. He would miss the way she hummed in the mornings, the way her laughter made him want to laugh, too. He would miss how her eyes sparkled when she looked at him, and the scent of her that filled each corner of the house. But, he wouldn't ask her to stay. He couldn't.

There was Samuel to consider. Cameron truly didn't know what to expect from the man. He'd thought he'd known Samuel once, believed he'd known the heart and soul of his old friend. But, all that had transpired proved him wrong. He hadn't known Samuel at all, and couldn't know what to anticipate if and when the man found him.

If, as he suspected, Samuel was coming for revenge, then Cameron didn't want Rebecca and Alicia anywhere near. He would never be able to live with himself if he knew that his past had in any way harmed Rebecca and Alicia.

Even if Samuel wasn't an issue, Cameron wouldn't ask Alicia to stay. He couldn't ask her to risk Rebecca's well-being just so he could have a live-in lover. And he certainly wasn't prepared to offer her any kind of permanent commitment.

He turned back and looked at her, remembering how she'd appeared when he'd first met her. Tense…hollow-eyed, exhausted…a month or so on the road and she would once again look like that.

Swiping a hand down his face in frustration, he wished there was something he could do to help her, a way to solve her problem so she could finally find peace, and a home and stability for herself and her daughter.

Monsters. They were everywhere. His was Samuel, a man he'd trusted and loved, a man who'd betrayed him. Alicia's monsters were in-laws, cold and autocratic and threatening to take away the one thing that mattered to her. Funny, that both of their monsters coveted something they had.

Again he turned back to the window and stared out into the arctic night. He wondered what had happened to Ginny. Where she had gone? If she had ever fallen in love and married?

He was surprised to discover there was no pain associated with thoughts of her. The pain had ebbed to nothing but a distant memory of an event that seemed oddly disconnected with him.

The ache in his heart had nothing to do with Ginny. He knew the ache was for Alicia. He thought of the trust fund money sitting in his account…enough to mount a custody battle defense, enough to possibly even the odds against Alicia's in-laws.

Hell, when the money had been embezzled by his sister's first husband, Cameron had written it off, assumed he'd never see it again.

When he'd received a portion of it back, he'd decided to keep it in the bank and build the ranch without it, the old-fashioned way with hard work and sweat. It sat in an account, doing nothing except drawing a little bit of interest.

Would she take it? Would she take the money and slay her monsters? Or would she keep running? He'd like to think she'd take it and defeat Broderick and Ruth Randall, stop running and build a life for herself and her daughter.

Of course it would be a life that didn't include him, but if he knew they were safe and happy, then it would be enough.

It would have to be.

He had his own problems to work out, his own monsters to defeat. He couldn't think beyond Samuel. He scanned the landscape, wondering when Samuel would come. He knew his old partner well. Samuel was almost phobic in his dislike of snowstorms. But, now the snow had stopped and soon he knew Samuel would show up.

"Cameron?"

He turned at the sound of Alicia's sleep-heavy voice. "Yeah?"

"Is everything all right?" Worry gave her voice a husky edge.

"Everything is fine." He left the window and went back to the side of the bed.

"Is it still snowing?" He felt her tension.

He hesitated a moment. "Yes. It's still snowing." It was a little white lie that hurt nobody. She sighed in relief. He slid back beneath the blankets and pulled her into his arms. "Go back to sleep," he said softly. And like an obedient child she closed her eyes, instantly falling back into the arms of slumber.

Chapter 12

"But I don't want to leave," Rebecca cried, her eyes filling with tears. "I like it here. I don't want to go anywhere else."

"Honey, I know you like it here, but we have to leave." Alicia placed an arm around Rebecca, trying to comfort her daughter while her own heart broke in half. "We knew eventually we'd have to leave here, that this wasn't our forever home."

"But 'ventally isn't here yet," Rebecca exclaimed, wiggling out of her mother's embrace. "I want to stay here. It's nice here and I have lots of new friends and I love Sugar."

"We'll find a place with another horse, one you'll love as much as Sugar," Alicia promised. Surely there were other ranches in other places where housekeeping help was needed. "And you can make new friends wherever we go."

Rebecca looked at her mother with tear-filled eyes. "But I love Mr. Lallager and we won't find another one of him."

Alicia drew Rebecca back into her arms and held her close, trying to stifle the tears that burned at her own eyes. "No, honey, no we won't," she agreed softly.

She'd known this moment was coming the instant she'd gotten out of bed and seen the sun shining brightly. The snowfall had stopped and a warm front had followed.

Throughout the morning the snow had begun to melt beneath the warming rays of the sun and by noon Alicia had been able to hear in the distance the sound of snowplows clearing the roads.

By three o'clock Wally had called to tell her that her car was ready to be picked up. Knowing to put off the inevitable for another day would only make things more difficult, Alicia had instructed Rebecca to start packing, that they would be leaving in an hour or so.

"Do we really have to go, Mommy?" Rebecca sniffled and swiped her eyes with the back of one hand. She looked so miserable, Alicia's heart broke yet again.

"Yes, honey, we really do."

With a sigh far too big, far too grown-up, Rebecca began packing her stuffed animals into their box. Alicia left to find Cameron to see if he would take them to their car.

He had already left her bed when she awakened that morning, and while the sun melted the snow, he'd been aloof and distant, as if they'd already gone from his mind, from his heart.

She found him in his study. Papers were strewn before him, but she had a feeling he wasn't focused on them. Surely he had to be thinking of Samuel, of the monster he would face all too soon.

"I'm sorry to bother you, but I was wondering if you would mind taking us into town to get my car."

"When?"

"As soon as we finish packing."

"So, you'll be leaving today?"

She nodded, a wind of despair blowing through her. Why did he have to look so damned handsome? Why did his eyes have to glow with that light that both thrilled and weakened her? She had slept in his arms last night and today she would tell him good-bye forever. She wondered if pain could cause death…because surely she hurt enough to die.

"Alicia…" He stood and picked something up from the top of his desk. "I want you to consider going back to Dallas, going back and trying to re-solve this mess you have."

"No." The word shot out of her sharply, without hesitation. "There is no resolution and I refuse to risk losing Rebecca."

He held out a check. "Maybe this will help you find some resolution."

With trembling fingers, she took it from him. She looked down at the amount, shocked as she saw the zeros that followed the fifty. "I…I can't take this." She looked at him in surprise.

"Please. I want you to have it, to fight for your

daughter.'' He smiled at the disbelief that still crossed her face. "Don't worry, it's good.'' His gaze caressed her face. "Take it, Alicia. Take it and solve the problem, then if there is anything left, build a life for yourself and Rebecca.''

Tears blurred her vision. His gesture of generosity only made her love for him ache more intensely in her heart. "Why? Why would you want to do this for me?''

He shoved his hands in his pockets and for a moment stared out the window. "I never really considered the money as mine. When my parents died, they left Elena and me a sizable trust fund. It was stolen, then recovered a couple of months ago. It's just been sitting in a bank vault growing dust. I want you to have it.''

"But you could do so much with it here. The house needs repairs, and the barn is in dismal shape. This kind of money would go a long way in building the kind of ranch you want.''

He smiled. "But I've always been a stubborn cuss. I prefer to build my ranch the hard way, like men have done for years and years before me. That's why the money hasn't been used already.''

She shook her head and held the check out to him. Her fingers trembled. "I can't take it, Cameron. I have no intention of going back to Dallas. It isn't just Broderick's money I'd be fighting, but also the power and influence that goes with the good old boy system of justice. Even with this money I couldn't win.''

He shoved his hands deeper in his pockets. "Keep

it in case you change your mind.'' He walked closer
to her, so close his nearness created an ache deep
inside her. ''You can't run forever, Alicia.''

But that's what she intended. To run forever, or
at least until Rebecca was old enough for Broderick
and Ruth's manipulations not to matter.

She looked at the check once again, and suddenly
her love for Cameron was too great, far too enormous to keep silent. ''I'm in love with you, Cameron.'' The words seeped out on a whisper. ''I love
you.''

She didn't give him an opportunity to reply, but
instead moved closer to him and leaned against his
chest. His heartbeat was thunder in her ears, and her
tears were the rain of hopelessness. ''Come with us,
Cameron. Come with me and Rebecca. We can find
another ranch, a place to build whatever you've
dreamed of. Don't stay here for Samuel to find.''

The words tumbled from her, born of desperation
and the love that pounded in her heart. ''I'm afraid
for you. Please…come with us.''

''Alicia.'' His voice was unusually deep, husky
as he placed his hands on her shoulders and gently
pulled her away from him. He cupped her face in
his hands. ''And what then? We build a life built
on lies, running from two monsters, your Broderick
and my Samuel?'' He shook his head and in his eyes
she saw her heart break. ''I care about you, Alicia,
but I can't go with you and you can't stay.''

She knew the truth of his words, and also registered the words he hadn't used. He hadn't said he
loved her, and a portion of her heart shattered into

a million little pieces. If she'd entertained any thoughts of staying any longer, they were dashed by the words he didn't speak.

"I'll let you know when we're ready to go." She turned and left before he could see the devastation in her eyes.

In her bedroom, she fought against a wave of tears, knowing she had to be strong for herself...and for Rebecca. It was good they were leaving now, before she had another day of loving Cameron, before she had any more nights of lying in his arms and feeling his heart beat against her own.

It took her only thirty minutes to pack up all that she had brought with her. There was only one thing she would be leaving without. A piece of her heart would always be here with Cameron.

With her bags ready to go, she went in to check on Rebecca's progress. The little girl was packed and sitting on her bed, staring out the window with a mournful expression. "All ready?" Alicia asked.

Rebecca sighed and nodded. With Cameron's help it took only a few minutes to load their bags and boxes into the back of the pickup, then they took off driving toward town.

The roads had been cleared, leaving huge snowdrifts on either side, but there were slick spots that forced Cameron to drive slow.

Rebecca was unnaturally quiet and Alicia realized the little girl had crawled back into the shell of isolation she'd worn when they first arrived.

Alicia stared out the window, filled with a hope-

lessness that knew no bounds. She and Rebecca
were back on the road to nowhere.

If only there was something she could use as leverage against Broderick and Ruth, one of those
skeletons Cameron had talked about. Again a vague
memory tried to surface, an obscure thought attempted to take shape.

She frowned thoughtfully. What was it that niggled at her? What struggled to be remembered…what thought begged to come to fruition?

She shook her head and placed a hand around
Rebecca as Cameron turned into the garage parking
area. Her car sat on the side of the building, ready
to take her and Rebecca away from Mustang, away
from Cameron.

While she paid the bill, Cameron loaded the trunk
of the car with their things. Rebecca stood near his
truck, silently watching him with huge, grieving
eyes.

By the time Alicia left the garage building, Cameron had finished loading them up. She stood, keys
in hand, looking at him, loving him.

Never had he looked more attractive. The daunt-
ing man who'd hired her was gone, replaced by the
man who owned her heart. "Cameron…I…" She
broke off, flushed, no words left to say.

Rebecca burst into tears and threw herself into
Cameron's arms. "I love you, Mr. Lallager," she
cried, her little arms wrapped around his neck.

He held her tight and closed his eyes for a long
moment. When he opened them again Alicia saw
the shine of tears and knew that even if he hadn't

been able to love her, he'd truly loved her daughter. Alicia was leaving a piece of her heart here with him, but Rebecca would be taking a piece of his when they left.

"And I love you, Rebecca," he said. He kissed her soundly on the cheek, then set her down on the ground.

"I wanted to stay with you forever," she said as she swiped free-falling tears. "I had my fingers double, double crossed that we could stay for always."

Cameron bent down and wiped her tears with his thumbs, much like he had wiped Alicia's. "Sometimes little girls have to pay for grown-up problems."

"But that's not fair," Rebecca said.

"I know, sweetheart, and I wish I could make it so life was always fair, but it's not." Cameron stood and gestured toward the car, his gaze on Alicia. "You'd better go before it gets any later. That radio of yours work?" She nodded. "Make sure you listen to the weather and don't try to drive in any Montana storms."

She nodded, wanting to scream. The weather. He was talking about the weather while her heart bled from mortal wounds. "Get in the car, Rebecca," she instructed. Rebecca, still silently crying, did as she was told.

Alicia quickly slid behind the steering wheel, not wanting to give him an opportunity to touch her in any way. If he touched her, she would crumble.

"Be safe, Cameron," she said as she started the engine.

He nodded, his eyes dark and fathomless. "And you be happy, Alicia," he replied.

She pulled out, fighting back tears.

Be happy. How was that possible without him in her life? How cruel fate had been to dangle a dream in front of her then cruelly snatch it away.

As she turned onto the highway that would take her out of Mustang, she looked into her rearview mirror, wanting one last look of the man she loved...the man she knew she would never see again.

Cameron watched the car until it disappeared from sight, a dull ache in the pit of his stomach. Already he felt the resounding emptiness of his house, the absence of laughter, of life.

She'd taken his check, but he knew she'd never cash it, knew she was headed for parts unknown, not back to Dallas to face her problems.

She was gone from his life now, and he should feel relieved. She had gotten too close, reached inside him where he hadn't allowed anyone in for a very long time. She'd been a threat. And yet he felt no relief now that she was gone. Only sadness and a loneliness deeper than any he'd ever felt before.

Irritated, he got into his truck and slammed the door. As he drove home he tried not to picture Rebecca's sweet face as she'd clung to his neck and told him she loved him. No matter what happened, Rebecca was the victim in the fight between Alicia and the Randalls.

He tightened his grip on the steering wheel as he

thought of Alicia's words of love to him. Beautiful Alicia with her sapphire eyes and the smile that warmed him throughout.

He knew she'd wanted words of love in return for her own, but he hadn't been able to speak of love, refused to believe he was capable of that emotion.

Once back at the ranch, he wandered from room to room, wishing the scent of her didn't linger, that the house didn't radiate with their very presence.

Rebecca's latest artwork still decorated the refrigerator door and one of Alicia's earrings remained on the cabinet, forgotten in the packing flurry.

He picked up the earring, a small gold hoop. She'd worn them the night of the Halloween party. She had dainty earlobes, and he remembered how she sighed in delight when he caught one of those lobes between his teeth. With a muttered curse, he tossed the earring into the trash.

He tensed as a knock fell on his front door. Had Alicia come back? Or had Samuel finally arrived? Somehow he couldn't believe that his nemesis would announce himself with an innocuous knock on the front door.

Moving to the window, he saw a familiar truck parked out front. He opened the door to find his sister and his brother-in-law on his front porch. In Elena's arms, Cameron's nephew grinned and drooled.

"Hi Cam. We stopped by to see how Alice and Rebecca survived their first snowstorm." She pointed to the melting snowman in the yard. "Looks like you all had some fun."

''They aren't here. They left...moved on.''

Elena stared at him first in confusion, then in disbelief. She turned and handed Trent the baby, then swept into the house as if to disprove his words. Trent shrugged and followed his wife into the living room. Cameron closed the front door and turned to face his sister.

''What do you mean they moved on? Cameron, what happened?'' She sank down on the sofa.

''Nothing happened. She decided she didn't like it here.'' He couldn't quite meet his sister's piercing gaze.

''I don't believe you. She was in love with you, Cameron.''

He sighed. ''I know, but she knew there was no future here. I'm not the kind of man she needs. You know me, Elena. I'm a loner.''

Elena stood and approached him. She reached up and touched his face. ''Oh, Cameron, how long do you intend to push people away from you? You can pretend with other people that you don't have a heart, but I know you too well to believe that. I've seen your heart and Alice saw it as well. It's not the heart of a loner.''

Cameron stepped away from her. ''Sometimes, dear sister, you're a real pain in the ass. Trent, I don't know how you put up with her.''

Trent smiled fondly at Elena and she returned his smile. ''Somehow I manage,'' he replied.

As Cameron saw the obvious love that existed between the two of them, a renewed pain of loss arrowed through him. Elena and Trent had the same kind of marriage Cameron's parents had enjoyed...one of mutual respect, passion and commitment.

By the time Elena and Trent left, Cameron had slid into a dark mood. As the sun set, he stalked out of the house and toward the stables, wanting to check on the horses. As always, Sugar greeted him with a friendly whinny and Bandit swished his tail and snorted a hello. And as always, the wild horse backed into a corner of her stall, ears flattened and nostrils flared.

Cameron stared at the horse, a proud beast who refused to bow to him. She had more spirit than any horse he'd ever seen and somehow she reminded him of Alicia.

It had taken Alicia a long time to trust him, to finally confide in him and he'd had to let her go. Perhaps it was time to let Mischief go as well.

Decision made, he opened the stall door, then propped open the wide doors that led outside. Knowing the horse wouldn't move while he was in sight, he walked around to the side of the stable and waited.

The sun had nearly disappeared when the horse bolted out of the stable. Her hooves thundered across the frozen ground as she headed out toward the distant pastures. The fencing in the pastures hadn't been completed, so Cameron knew eventually she'd find her way back to the box canyon where he'd caught her, back to the pack where she belonged. Eventually she'd find her way home.

He walked back to the house, an emptiness inside

him. As he stepped through the front door, the phone rang. He hurried to answer.

"Hi Cameron." Alicia's voice washed over him, momentarily easing the yawning emptiness. "I wanted to call and tell you that you were right."

"Right about what?" He sat on the sofa and gripped the receiver tightly against his ear.

"It's time to stop running."

He heard the sound of her breathing, then she continued. "I'm going home, back to Dallas to face my monsters."

He closed his eyes, imagining her fear, the courage it had taken for her to come to such a decision. "I'm glad, Alicia."

"I...I just wanted to thank you for everything and tell you if I do use your check, I promise I'll pay you back every cent."

"That isn't necessary. It was a gift, not a loan."

"No. I'll pay you back. It's the only way I can accept."

"Okay," he agreed. He wanted to think of something to say, some reason to keep her on the line so he could hear her voice a little longer. But he had no words left, nothing to offer her.

"Well...I just wanted to tell you what I'd decided," she hesitated a moment, then continued. "I'll be in touch about the money. Goodbye." She hung up quickly, as if knowing there was nothing more to say.

So, she was going home. Back to Dallas to fight the Randalls. Good, it was the only way she could live a normal life, the only way she could give Rebecca a good life. She'd run long enough. She had to face those monsters.

He leaned his head back and closed his eyes, wondering how long it would be before he faced his own.

Chapter 13

Alicia and Rebecca had driven for several hours in the direction of Wyoming. They stopped for the night in an inexpensive, but clean motel along the highway.

"Will it always be like this, Mommy?" Rebecca had asked as they carried their suitcases into the small, stale-smelling room. "Will we ever have a real home again?"

It was then that Alicia had made her decision to return to Dallas and face whatever fate had in store for her. The thought of losing Rebecca was intolerable, but the life Alicia was giving her daughter on the run was almost as bad.

She loved Rebecca enough to risk going home and seeing if there wasn't some sort of arrangement that could be worked out with the Randalls.

If worse came to worse, she had the check from

Cameron to use to hire a decent lawyer to fight a court battle.

Rebecca had almost immediately fallen asleep, exhausted by the emotional turmoil of the day, and it was then that Alicia had called Cameron.

She wasn't sure what had prompted the call. She told herself he had a right to know her plans, but she suspected the truth was she wanted…needed to hear his voice just one last time. And someplace deep in her heart, she'd hoped he'd tell her he missed her, he wanted her to come back, that he loved her. But of course that hadn't happened.

Minutes later she lay in the motel bed, her thoughts whirling in her head. Cameron's voice had caressed her, the deep tones both a pleasure and a torment. She'd had to fight with herself not to pack Rebecca back into the car, turn around and drive back to Mustang, to him.

But to what purpose? She'd told him she loved him, and he'd said he cared about her. Cared. Like she had for Robert. But caring and the kind of love she felt for Cameron were two very different emotions. And just as she knew now that caring about Robert would have never been enough for her had he lived, she knew Cameron caring for her would never be enough for her.

She turned over on the lumpy bed, seeking a more comfortable position as her mind whirled. Again she had the feeling that she'd forgotten something important…something about Robert and the day of his unexpected death.

Poor Robert. He'd wanted so desperately to break

away from his parents, but years of conditioning by them had made him feel inept and afraid. He knew he and Alicia would lose everything if he separated from them...the house, his job, their comfortable way of living. Torn between his desire to support Alicia and Rebecca and the crushing power of his parents, Robert had plunged into a depression where nothing seemed possible.

She frowned and closed her eyes, willing her thoughts to take her back to the day of his death. The shock and grief of his accident had obscured much of the events of that day in her mind. But she now felt it vitally important that she remember every minute.

The week before the accident, Robert had seemed unusually happy...excited and several times he told Alicia he was working on something that just might help him create a different future for them. Although Alicia had questioned him several times for details, he'd merely smiled and told her to be patient.

What had he been working on? Were there skeletons in the Randall family closet as Cameron had suggested? Whatever it was, Robert was a man who wrote down everything, kept records of phone calls, both business and personal.

His briefcase.

Alicia sat up with a gasp. The police had released the briefcase to her, but she'd been too distraught at the time to even think about looking in it.

What had she done with it? Where had she put it? Dammit, she couldn't remember.

She stretched out once again, knowing there was

nothing she could do until she got back to Dallas. Hopefully the house would still be just as she'd left it. Hopefully Broderick and Ruth hadn't cleaned the place out and sold it.

Closing her eyes, she ached for Cameron's arms around her. She wondered if the pain of the betrayal he'd suffered at Ginny and Samuel's hands had made it impossible for him to ever love again. If so, it was sad.

She knew that Cameron had a wealth of love trapped inside him, love that escaped when he was with Rebecca and when he made love to Alicia.

Somehow she'd hoped she'd be the one to heal him, to make him want to trust in love again, but that hadn't happened. The most she could hope for was that another woman would come along for him, one who would finally make him give himself completely, one with whom he would build a family and live happily-ever-after.

Tears oozed out from beneath her eyelids. If she couldn't bring him a lifetime of happiness, then the next best thing she could do was wish that life for him with another woman.

And perhaps when enough time had passed, she would forget the time she'd spent in Mustang and the love she'd left behind.

She and Rebecca hit the road just after dawn the next morning, each mile taking them closer to Dallas and uncertainty.

Alicia had awakened without the normal jangle of nerves, without the fear that she'd lived with for the past several months. Instead a cold, hard resolve had formed in her chest, bringing with it a strange kind of serenity.

Her decision to face whatever lay ahead was the right one. No more running, no more furtive glances over her shoulder, no more fear.

Somehow, someway, she would fight Broderick and Ruth and win. She had to believe that…she had to believe that ultimately good always prevails over evil, that God wouldn't allow her daughter to be raised by coldhearted, dictatorial monsters.

That night once again they slept in a cheap, non-descript motel. Alicia fought with herself, wanting to pick up the phone and once again hear Cameron's voice, feel his closeness even if just for a moment over impersonal phone lines. She fell asleep only after hours of tossing and turning.

The next morning she and Rebecca continued their journey just after dawn. The sunrise promised a beautiful day, but Alicia couldn't take pleasure in the colorful explosion of the awakening day.

As she drove, her thoughts alternated between the confrontation to come and Cameron. There was no way to prepare herself for what was to come, and she hadn't been prepared for how many times in each moment memories of Cameron drifted into her head.

Cameron, with his slow, sexy smile and dark eyes that lit flames inside Alicia. Cameron, whose laughter reached inside her to pluck at heartstrings. His vision danced before her, his deep voice a recurring echo in her head.

Even Rebecca seemed to have trouble removing

Cameron from their life. "Mr. Lallager was the best-est cowboy in the whole world," she told Alicia as they ate lunch in a hamburger joint. She clicked the heels of her boots together, like Dorothy in Oz trying to get home. "He boughtted me these boots because he loved me." Childish blue eyes looked at Alicia as if for confirmation.

"That's right, honey. Mr. Gallagher loved you very much and he was a wonderful cowboy."

Rebecca picked up a French fry. Again she looked at her mother. "Mr. Lallager loved me almost as much as daddy, didn't he?"

Alicia nodded, her throat too filled with emotion for words.

"Will we ever see Mr. Lallager again?"

Alicia swallowed hard, but the lump in her throat refused to dislodge. "I don't know, honey," she finally managed to reply.

She refused to give Rebecca false hope, refused to entertain it herself. For all practical purposes, Cameron Gallagher was out of their lives forever.

If she ended up spending the money he'd given her, then eventually when she got on her feet, she would return the money in regular monthly payments and that would be the extent of their contact.

As they entered the city limits of Dallas, Alicia tightened her grip on the steering wheel. Within minutes they would be at the house she'd shared with Robert...a house just down the street from Broderick and Ruth's home.

She was now in the monsters' territory and the nerves that had been silent all day now screamed inside of her. She glanced over at Rebecca, grateful the little girl had fallen asleep.

Alicia leaned over and opened the glove compartment. Rummaging around inside, her fingers closed on the small, square garage door opener. She pulled it out and placed it on the seat next to her.

She hoped nobody had changed the locks, prayed that she could pull into the garage and nobody would know they were in the house. She needed time…time to form a plan, time to search for the briefcase that might hold some answers. She didn't want Broderick and Ruth to know they were back in the house until she was ready to confront them.

Taking the exit that led to their development, her heart beat increased, pounding painfully in her chest. Please…don't let this be a mistake, she prayed. Her worst nightmare was that the police would show up at her door, place her under arrest for some manufactured reason, and Rebecca would be taken to Broderick and Ruth's and Alicia would never see her again.

She shivered and fought the impulse to turn the car around, go back on the run. No more. The life she was giving Rebecca by running wasn't healthy, and Alicia loved her daughter enough to take the chance of a lifetime.

Her heart rocked in her chest as she turned a corner and the house came into view. It looked just as it had when they'd left—a stately two-story red brick, rather cold in appearance.

At the end of a cul-de-sac the Randall home rose up like a feudal castle. The dozens of windows looked like large, staring eyes, and Alicia prayed nobody stood at them, peering out as she pulled into the driveway of her home.

She punched the garage door opener and gasped in relief as the door slid soundlessly open. She pulled into the empty garage, shut off the car engine and quickly hit the button again, allowing the door to close behind them.

For a long moment she sat, listening to the ticking of the cooling engine, Rebecca's soft, regular breathing, and the slowing of her own heart beat. She would know within minutes if anyone saw her pull in.

Two minutes. Three minutes. Five…ten. After fifteen minutes had passed and nothing happened, Alicia awakened Rebecca and together the two entered the house they'd left behind when they'd begun their life on the run.

Somebody had been in the house since she'd been gone. The food had been taken out of the refrigerator and her plants were all healthy and recently watered.

Rebecca immediately ran up the wide staircase to her room, where many of her toys and stuffed animals had been left behind. Alicia walked around the kitchen, into the living room, touching a piece of furniture here, another item there, orienting herself to the past.

Despite the expensive furniture, the amenities of living, this place had never felt like a real home. Everything had been bought and paid for by Broderick and Ruth, and Alicia had always felt as if she were living in a borrowed house, surrounded by things that didn't really belong to her.

Cameron's house, with its scuffed-up walls and worn furniture had embraced her with warmth, with the feel of belonging. But of course, that had been a false aura, for Cameron didn't love her and so she could never really belong in his home.

"Stop it," she demanded to herself. She had to stop thinking of him, needed to focus on what she could do, not what she couldn't change.

Robert's briefcase. She had to find it, see what he'd been up to before his death. Somehow she felt that the answers to her problems with Broderick and Ruth were contained in the leather case. And if she found the briefcase and the answers to her problems weren't there, then she needed to think…somehow figure out a way to beat the monsters who plagued her.

The note was tacked on Bandit's stall in the stable.

Meet me at dusk in the grove of trees near the pond.

It was signed Samuel.

Cameron tore the note down and tucked it into his pocket, his gaze scanning the stable area for evidence that he was not alone.

He wasn't sure when Samuel had been here, but he was certain his old partner was no longer anywhere near. The horses were too calm for a stranger to be in the immediate vicinity.

Finally. Finally contact had been made and he knew where and when he'd face Samuel and whatever rage the man brought with him.

After feeding the horses, he went back into the house and into his bedroom. In the drawer at the top of his dresser, he pulled out a small box, and inside the box was his nine-millimeter gun.

He hadn't had it out since his days of bounty hunting. He hadn't thought he'd ever need to get it out again. But there was no way he'd go unarmed to meet Samuel.

He carried the gun, ammunition and cleaning equipment to the kitchen table. Making sure the gun was unloaded, he proceeded to clean it.

As he worked, the silence of the kitchen pressed around him. And in the silence came thoughts of Alicia.

She and Rebecca should be in Dallas by now. He hoped things worked out for her, that she could somehow solve the problem of her in-laws and settle down to a normal, happy life.

Hopefully one day she'd find a good man who would love her and be a father to Rebecca, the kind of man they deserved, a man far different from him.

He frowned, trying to shove away a mental picture of Alicia in another man's arms, Alicia tasting another man's lips. These mental images created a hard knot of tension in the pit of his stomach.

He had to stop thinking about her, needed to focus solely on the imminent confrontation with Samuel.

Samuel.

Cameron had last seen the man the day law enforcement officials, Jack Heggar and Cameron had
set up a sting. Using an undercover cop as a felon
in hiding, cameras had caught Samuel receiving a
payoff from the supposed felon. Law officers had
moved in and placed Samuel under arrest. At that
time, Samuel had spewed threats, most of them
pointed directly at Cameron.

Samuel's arrest had taken place three days after
Cameron had caught Samuel and Ginny in bed together. Two weeks before Cameron had surprised
them in bed, Cameron had begun the process of seeing Samuel arrested, unable to condone the illegal
activity the man was committing. But, Cameron
knew that Samuel believed his arrest had been the
direct result of Cameron learning about Samuel's
betrayal with Ginny.

"You son-of-a-bitch," Samuel had yelled as he'd
been handcuffed and led away. "A man would have
settled this by coming to me, by talking to
Ginny…but only a good for nothing rat would take
it this far. I'll get you, Gallagher. Sooner or later,
I'll get you for this."

And now that time had arrived. Cameron allowed
his thoughts to take him back to that moment in time
when he'd stepped through his bedroom door and
seen his best friend and his girlfriend tangled together.

He needed the anger that the memory evoked,
needed to remember the hatred he'd felt at that moment for the man who was his best friend.

The anger would make him strong enough to face whatever rage Samuel brought with him. The anger charged his adrenaline and sent it flowing hot through his veins. But more than anything, the anger shoved away any thoughts of Alicia, any memories that touched a sweet, soft place in his heart. He couldn't afford any softness…not if he wanted to stay alive.

At least Samuel hadn't sneaked up on him or shot him through a window. Somehow that didn't surprise Cameron. Samuel would cuckold him, but would prefer a fair fight to a sneak attack.

It was the longest day of Cameron's life as he waited for sunset. With the gun in a holster around his waist, he prowled the rooms of the house, trapped in memories both painful and pleasant.

As the sun started its descent in the western sky, Cameron headed out for the pond and the grove of trees where he would meet his past.

He walked with determined footsteps, ready to meet whatever lay ahead. He realized as he approached the large stand of thick trees that every day for the past two years someplace in the back of his mind he had known this day would come.

The knowledge that sooner or later he would have to face Samuel had colored every day, every event, every emotion he'd entertained in the past two years.

It was almost a relief to finally know that the end was near, that closure, one way or another was just ahead of him.

The snow had melted in the past two days, lingering only along the northwestern sides of buildings and trees where little daylight shone. Cameron's footsteps sunk slightly into the thawing ground, but he knew how to walk to make as little noise as possible.

By the time he reached the grove of trees, his adrenaline soared and his heart beat a slow rhythm of control. He knew Samuel was here, knew it by the prickling at the base of his skull, knew it by the faintest scent of shaving cream that rode on the evening air.

Cameron stood just at the edge of the trees, his back to the wide open pasture behind him. He pulled his gun, reassured by the familiar weight and cool metal of the weapon. "Samuel."

Samuel Blankenship stepped out from behind a nearby tree, a gun in his hand as he faced Cameron.

The two years in prison had not been kind to Samuel. He was thinner than Cameron had ever seen him and a livid scar decorated one cheek. But his eyes were the same…green eyes lit with humor.

Cameron wasn't fooled by the amusement in Samuel's eyes. He'd seen that same expression as Samuel broke a man's jaw in a bar fight, had seen that sparkle as Samuel was arrested and led away. Samuel had always had that impish gleam in his eyes, as if life were a big joke and he intended to have the final laugh.

"Cameron." He nodded his head slightly in greeting. He touched the scar on his cheek. "As you can see, bounty hunters aren't exactly popular in prison. They rank up there with cops and other law enforcement professionals."

Cameron said nothing, but merely tightened his grip on his gun, unsure what to expect.

For an endless moment they faced each other, guns held steady, eyes narrowed. A million thoughts and countless memories swept through Cameron's head.

Their shared laughter at the time when he and Samuel had been chasing a fugitive and Samuel had gotten the seat of his pants ripped by a German shepherd's teeth.

He remembered his gratefulness when Samuel had nursed him when he'd developed a vicious bout of the flu and later he'd returned the favor when Samuel had come down with the same symptoms.

Partners…friends…brothers, and now they faced each other over the barrels of their guns. Sorrow swept through Cameron, a sorrow achingly sharp and completely unexpected.

How had it come to this? How had brotherly love turned to hatred? How had two friends come to face each other with weapons doing their talking?

With a sigh of irritation, Cameron threw his gun to the ground, knowing he could never pull the trigger while it was aimed at Samuel. "I don't know why you're here, Samuel. If it's to kill me, then be done with it."

"Hell, I don't want to kill you, Cam." Samuel's gun hit the ground. "I just want to talk to you, get some things off my chest before I move on."

"I don't figure we have anything to talk about," Cameron replied, wanting the man to leave, just to go away and never be heard from again.

"We do have something to talk about. We need to talk about Ginny."

Cameron snorted. "What's to say? Last time I saw her she was in my bed...with you." He stared at Samuel with an accusatory glare. "Good God, Samuel. You were my best friend, and she was my girl."

Samuel gazed at the ground, as if unable to meet Cameron's eyes. "I know." He leaned back against a tree trunk and raked a hand through his sandy hair. "Neither one of us meant for it to happen, Cam. But you were always pushing us together, encouraging us to spend time together." Samuel looked at Cameron. "You have to take on some of the responsibility for what happened. You didn't want her. You never really loved her."

Cameron opened his mouth to protest, self-righteous anger coursing through him. Just as quickly the kernel of truth in Samuel's words sank in.

Five weeks ago, before Alicia's presence in his life, Cameron would have fought Samuel on the point, insisting that he'd loved Ginny. But now, with Alicia in his heart, he knew Samuel spoke the truth.

"I loved her, Cameron. I still love Ginny." Samuel sighed and once again tore a hand through his hair. "Hell Cameron, we both loved you and neither of us wanted to hurt you. We made the mistake of falling in love with each other. We didn't plan it, we fought against it for as long as we could." Samuel's eyes were dark and tortured. "We didn't want to hurt you, Cameron," he repeated. "We never wanted that."

Cameron waved his hand impatiently. "Aside from all that, you could have gotten me killed…you could have gotten us both killed by telling fugitives when we were coming. We could have easily been set up." Cameron's anger rose as he thought of Samuel's exploitation of him and the system they worked for. "Dammit, Samuel, you were gambling with our lives."

"I know. But at the time I wasn't thinking with my head." Again Samuel sighed, the sigh of regret, of grief for past wrongs and present hurts. "Let's face it, Cameron. You're a hell of a lot more handsome than me. The women always flocked to you. Wherever we went, you were the one the women looked at, wanted."

Cameron waved his hand again in frustration. "What in the hell does that have to do with you taking payoffs?"

"I couldn't believe that Ginny would love me just for me. I figured the way to hold her was to have enough money to grant her every wish." Samuel frowned and rubbed a hand across his wrinkled brow. "I didn't give her enough credit, and I damn straight didn't give myself enough credit."

Cameron released a sigh that held two years of pain, two years of anger. He suddenly realized his pain hadn't been so much about Ginny and Samuel's betrayal. He looked at the man he'd once loved like family. "What hurt more than anything, Samuel, was that you expected me to go along with you, you expected me to keep my mouth shut about your crimes.''

Again a knot of anger hardened and grew in Cameron's stomach, making him feel half-ill. ''Dammit man, you tried to steal my honor, to take away my ethics. And that hurt more than your deception where Ginny was concerned.''

Samuel nodded, the corners of his mouth pulled down with regret. ''I'd lost all my honor, gave it away because I thought I had to in order to hold Ginny. I was wrong, Cameron, and I'll never be able to go back and change things.''

Samuel's frown fell away and he gazed at Cameron with an expression of awe. ''She loves me, and she's waited for me. For two years, she's waited. We're going to put the past behind us and be happy. But before we start our life together, I needed to talk to you, needed to tell you I'm sorry for all of it.''

Put the past behind. Cameron felt the pieces of his heart that had been frozen for so long starting to thaw. Samuel and Ginny had fallen in love, and Cameron couldn't fault them for that.

Samuel was right, Cameron had never loved Ginny. There had been a time when she'd begged him for a commitment and he'd refused. Was it any wonder she'd looked elsewhere? And could he really blame them for finding what they needed in each other?

He knew there was no way to guard a heart against love. He'd sworn he'd live his life alone, never love again, and somehow Alicia had crawled beneath his defenses and penetrated the very core of his soul.

The love he'd denied, refused to acknowledge suddenly filled him up, warming the last of the cold places of his heart.

Alicia. He loved her. Alicia. He needed her. Sweet Alicia. He'd let her go.

Cameron looked at the man he'd believed he hated, the man who had once been his friend. Although he knew they could never get back what had been lost, his anger and sense of betrayal were gone, leaving only a deep sadness and the memory of a man who had once been his friend.

"Apology accepted," Cameron said and held out his hand.

Samuel grabbed the outstretched hand and the two men shook. Peace flowed through Cameron and he knew his monster had been slayed, not by violence, but by forgiveness.

"Be happy, Cameron," Samuel said as he released Cameron's hand.

"That's exactly what I intend to do," Cameron replied. He grabbed his gun from the ground, tucked it back into his holster, then turned and sprinted back toward the house, knowing for the first time exactly what it would take for him to be happy. Alicia.

Chapter 14

Throughout the remainder of the day and into early evening Alicia hunted for Robert's briefcase. While Rebecca played quietly in her room with the toys she'd been unable to take with her on their travels, Alicia ransacked the house, seeking the elusive attaché case.

When darkness fell, Alicia was reluctant to turn on any lights, not wanting to alert any neighbors, especially Broderick and Ruth, of their presence in the house. Instead, she and Rebecca played cards by flashlight until it was time to tuck Rebecca into bed.

With Rebecca asleep, Alicia continued the search, growing more desperate with each minute that passed. She finally sank down on the sofa in the darkness of the living room, wondering if returning had been a mistake. The check Cameron had given her was a lot of money, but was it enough to mount a defense against a couple who were probably millionaires?

There were a hundred ways to bleed a fund when fighting a court battle, and Alicia had a feeling the Randalls would know all of them.

She leaned her head forward and pressed two fingers against an eyebrow, where tension worked overtime to produce a headache. Tears burned, tears of frustration, of exhaustion and finally the tears she'd held in since leaving Mustang…tears for Cameron and what would never be.

She gave in to them, wrapping her arms around herself and rocking back and forth, her heart aching with an intense pain she'd never felt before.

So, this was heartbreak. She'd felt immense sadness when Robert had died, ached for her daughter who would grow up without her father, but her heart hadn't hurt like this. This ache sliced through her, like the coldest wind on the chilliest winter day.

When the tears finally stopped their trek down her cheeks, she once again faced the problem at hand. Cameron couldn't help her now…even if he were here, this was a problem she had to solve herself, demons she had to slay in order to be truly free.

Rebecca's room. It came to her suddenly, without effort. She remembered now. She'd come home from the police station, where they had given her Robert's belongings. Needing to hold her daughter, she'd gone right into Rebecca's room and set the briefcase next to the bed. As she'd held Rebecca, rocking her and explaining about death and Heaven, she'd kicked the briefcase out of her way. It had skidded beneath the bed.

Holding the flashlight tight, praying her memory didn't deceive her, Alicia crept into Rebecca's room and got down on her hands and knees. Peering beneath the bed, she spied the errant attaché case. As quietly as possible she pulled it out and left the bedroom.

As she carried the case into the kitchen, she flipped the brass fasteners, stifling a moan of frustration as they refused to release. Locked. Dammit. Why was everything so damned difficult?

She placed the briefcase on the kitchen table and retrieved a knife from the drawer. It took her nearly thirty minutes of prying and jiggling to finally pop the locks and open the case.

With trembling hands, she pulled out the papers that rested inside. Using the flashlight, she picked up the first sheet of paper and began reading.

Business reports. A day planner. Copies of memos from Robert to his secretary, Paige. Alicia read each and every item word for word, despair once again rising up inside her.

She'd hoped. She'd prayed that somehow the answers would be here. With her heart pounding anxiously, she pulled the last item out of the briefcase, a slim manila folder with Randall Electronics written across the front. Probably another business report of some kind, she thought as she flipped the folder open.

It wasn't a business report. She frowned as she read the cover letter written to Robert from a Jim

Casey of Casey's Investigative Enterprises. It appeared to be a letter confirming an investigation begun on Robert's behalf. An investigation of what?

She set the letter aside and picked up the next piece of paper, a photocopy of a page from an old newspaper. The article was about a man named Henry Brockburn, a medical doctor convicted of selling babies in a black market scheme.

Why would Robert care about this? What could this doctor have to do with Alicia's husband? As she looked at the date of the article, her heart beat an unsteady rhythm. The doctor had been arrested three years after Robert was born. Was it possible? Could it be?

The last item in the folder gave her the answer. Tears filled her eyes as she realized she held the key to her freedom. There was no way Broderick and Ruth would want this information to become public.

Triumph soared through Alicia. Yes, this was it. This had to be it. This was what Robert had been working on...this was the information that he'd known would gain them their freedom from Broderick and Ruth.

Her hands trembled as she pressed the papers against her chest. Now she understood Robert's euphoria the week before he died. The knowledge contained here would have helped break his emotional ties, and the threat of creating a scandal would have permitted Robert to walk away with some sort of monetary settlement.

Alicia didn't want a settlement. She didn't care about the Randall money. She just wanted them out of her life…out of Rebecca's life. Carefully she placed the items back in the folder. "This is my ticket to freedom," she said aloud. And first thing in the morning, she intended to face her monsters, armed with the truth as her only weapon.

Sleep seemed to have taken a leave of absence. She stretched out in the bed she had shared with Robert, but her thoughts were not of him, but of another man.

Cameron. When did the hurt stop? When would she be able to think of his name and not ache with want…with need? She'd gone to Mustang to find a place to hide, she'd never dreamed she'd lose her heart there.

At least something good had come from her heartbreak and her trip to Mustang. If not for Cameron encouraging her to face her monsters she would have never come back here, never found the information that would make her free forever.

Sleep finally came, embracing her in dreamless slumber. She awakened at six the next morning, eager to confront Broderick and Ruth and put the past behind her forever. Only with the past behind her could she face her future…a future of rebuilding…a future without Cameron. She shoved this thought out of her mind. She couldn't dwell any longer on what would never be.

Dressed and armed with a cup of coffee, she picked up the phone and dialed Broderick and Ruth's house. The maid answered. "Emma, this is Alicia. I want to speak to Broderick."

A stunned silence greeted her words. "I'll...I'll see if he's available," Emma stuttered in surprise.

"Oh, I'm certain he'll be available," Alicia replied dryly.

"Where in the hell are you?" Broderick's voice boomed across the line.

"That's the problem with having a maid to answer your phone instead of caller ID." Alicia tried to still her quivering nerves.

"Dammit, I'm not playing games here. Where's my granddaughter?" He drew an audible breath, as if attempting to swallow some of his anger. "Alicia, be reasonable. You and Rebecca need our help. Let's sit down and talk. I'm sure we can work something out."

Alicia wasn't fooled by his conciliatory tone. She knew the man could smooth talk a snake, at the same time he was stealing the snake's skin. "Yes," she agreed. "I want to talk to you and Ruth. I'd like to come to the house in an hour."

"Fine...fine," Broderick readily agreed. "I'm sure we can come to some sort of agreement where Rebecca is concerned."

Alicia didn't reply. She knew exactly what sort of agreement he had in mind...that she bow out of her daughter's life and let them raise Rebecca. "I'll see you in an hour," she said, then disconnected.

An hour. In an hour her life would change. It would either get better, or it would deteriorate beyond repair. Oh, how she wanted to call Cameron, tell him she was about to confront her monsters and she was frightened. How she wished he were here to hold her up, to hide behind.

But she couldn't hide any longer. She couldn't continue to drag her daughter from small town to small town, constantly afraid, continually on edge. It was time for change and one way or the other she would be strong enough to face whatever came. If Cameron could face his past with Samuel, then Alicia could face her own fate.

She woke up Rebecca and as the little girl dressed, Alicia's thoughts once again went to Cameron. Was he all right? She had to believe he was…that if Samuel had found him no harm had come to him. She had to believe that Cameron faced his monster and won because that gave her strength to face her own.

"How would you like to go to Nancy's Day Care for a little while this morning?" Alicia asked her daughter as Rebecca pulled on her cowboy boots.

"Okay. I like Ms. Nancy," Rebecca agreed. Rebecca had occasionally spent time at the nearby day-care center and had developed a real fondness for the young woman who ran the business.

"Mommy?" Rebecca's boots clicked against the floor as she walked over to where Alicia sat on the edge of the bed.

"What, honey?" Alicia pulled Rebecca's little body into her arms.

"I don't want to stay in this house. I don't like it here."

Alicia kissed Rebecca's cheek and hugged her tight. She knew why Rebecca didn't like it here.

This house was far too close to the grandparents who frightened Rebecca, grandparents who had actively sought to alienate Rebecca from her mother.

"We'll only be here for the day, then we're going to find a place and settle down, a place where we can have our own home and not move anymore."

Rebecca nodded. "Can we move to Mustang so I can see Mr. Lallager every day?"

Aching pain swept through Alicia. If only he'd loved her. "No sweetie, but we'll find a town just as nice, a town with cowboys."

Rebecca sighed and Alicia knew the little girl was wrestling with her own kind of heartbreak. But little girl hearts healed far easier than grown-up ones. There was no way Alicia could go back to Mustang, see Cameron every day and not feel her soul dying a slow death.

All too soon, it was time for Alicia to leave. She drove Rebecca to the day care, kissed her on the cheek and promised to be back soon. As she drove back she prayed she wasn't walking into a trap.

If Broderick and Ruth had already somehow received a judgment of custody and Alicia had been proclaimed a fugitive from justice, then it was possible Alicia could be arrested. And if that happened, she had no idea what she'd do.

She slowed her car as she approached her house. A car sat in the driveway. Her heart pounded in a flurry of nervous anxiety. Was it the police? Had Broderick figured out that she was at the house and sent the authorities to pick her up?

In an instant she had to make a decision. Stop?

Or drive by the house and continue on to the Randall mansion at the end of the street. She slowed and the sole occupant of the car opened the driver door and stood.

Tall, lanky, with a dark cowboy hat that was achingly familiar. Cameron. Alicia slammed on the brakes and whirled into the driveway. She was out of the car before the motor completely stopped running.

"Cameron." She checked the impulse to race to him, to throw herself into his arms. "Wha...what are you doing here? How did you find me?"

He walked toward her, an easy smile curving his lips. "You weren't hard to find. Your husband's name and address is listed in the phone book. I flew in, rented the car and only had to ask for directions a couple of times."

"But...but what are you doing here?" She searched his features, trying to still the thundering of her heart.

He shrugged, his gaze studying her intently. "I thought maybe you might need some moral support. What's going on with your in-laws? Is there going to be a court battle?"

Moral support. She wanted to thank him for caring, but it hurt that he hadn't said he loved her, he needed her, he couldn't live without her. She shoved the hurt away and focused on the last of his questions. "I'm not sure. I was on my way to talk to Ruth and Broderick when I saw your car."

"Where's Rebecca?"

"I just dropped her off at a day care. I didn't want her with me for the confrontation."

"Want me there for the confrontation?"

His presence confused her, but she couldn't focus on that right now. She had to keep her thoughts schooled to the matter at hand…to facing Broderick and Ruth. "I'd love it," she replied, knowing she could face anything if she knew Cameron was beside her.

At the moment it didn't matter that he didn't love her like she wanted him to. It was enough that he was here. "I found the skeletons," she said a moment later as they pulled into the Randall driveway.

"I'm glad." His deep voice swept over her, through her and she felt a renewed burst of strength. She shut off the engine and stared at the front door of the Randall mansion. Inside lay her future, Rebecca's future.

There had been a moment in time when she'd thought perhaps her future lay with the man sitting next to her. Although her heart would always ache for what might have been with Cameron, she also felt eternal gratitude, for if not for him, she wouldn't be here taking her future into her own hands.

"You okay?" he asked.

She nodded, grateful that he didn't touch her. She had a feeling if he touched her in any way, she'd shatter into a million little pieces.

"Let's go," she said grimly. She got out of the car and strode to the front door, her shoulders stiffened in grim determination. In the purse she carried were the papers she'd found in Robert's briefcase...papers she hoped were the key to her freedom.

Emma answered Alicia's knock, her gaze flaring slightly as she took in Cameron's presence. She opened the door to allow them entry. "You are to wait in the library. Mr. and Mrs. Broderick will be with you momentarily."

The library. It was the room where Alicia and Robert had first told Broderick and Ruth of their marriage...a room that held nothing but bad memories. "Tell them we'll wait in the front living room," Alicia said and swept past Emma into the formal living area where she'd rarely been in the past, a room rarely used by the Randalls.

She refused to give Broderick the upper hand, refused to meet him on turf mired in bad memories. Emma emitted a resigned sigh as she hurried from the room.

Alicia drew a deep breath, all thoughts of Cameron shoved away as she readied herself for the battle to come.

Cameron stood just inside the room as Alicia paced back and forth on the Oriental carpet. He had felt the chill in the house the moment he'd entered. Not a temperature coolness, but the lack of love, of compassion, of utter humanity.

He tried to imagine Alicia's life with the people who lived here, but he couldn't. Alicia was far too filled with warmth, embodied with a life spirit that didn't belong in this cold place.

His first impulse when he'd seen her had been to

sweep her up in his arms, proclaim his love for her and take her back to Mustang where she belonged. But he'd seen the shadows in her eyes, knew she was still chained to her past, and until that issue was resolved, she'd never really be free.

As she paced back and forth he felt her distance from him, and it stirred a growing uneasiness in him. If she managed to settle the custody issue with the Randalls, would she still be in love with him?

When she'd told him she loved him, she'd been on the run, frightened and alone. Vulnerable. And in that particular state, it would be easy to mistake affection for love, the need to be held and supported for passion.

The thought of not having Alicia in his life swept a cold wind through him. She'd brought him to life, made him recognize just how lonely, how isolated he'd been. He didn't want to go back to that forsaken, solitary life.

However, he knew there was nothing he could do for Alicia now. Just as he'd had to face his past and resolve it, so did she. And she had to do it alone. All he could do was be here for her when it was finished…if it finished.

"He's doing this on purpose," she said softly as she stopped her frantic pacing. "He's making me wait to psych me out. He's a master at mind games. But it's not working." She clutched her purse tightly against her chest. "He can't bully me or manipulate me any longer."

Cameron nodded, proud of the strength he saw radiating from her eyes. But he'd known it was there, had seen her spirit so many times in his time with her.

At that moment Broderick and Ruth entered the room. Broderick Randall was a big man, dressed as a caricature of a Texan. Clad in a white western shirt with a belt buckle the size of a dinner plate, the man looked like an overstuffed, overfed pompous buffoon, but when Cameron looked into his eyes, he recognized that this man was nobody's fool. Broderick Randall's blue eyes radiated craftiness, intelligence and held a soulless quality.

Ruth Randall was perfectly coiffed and clad in an expensive dress with a string of pearls at her throat. Her face had the strained, taut features of a woman who'd had one too many face-lifts in an attempt to retain her youth.

"Where in the hell have you been?" Broderick greeted Alicia, then turned to Cameron. "And who in the hell are you?"

"Cameron is a friend," Alicia replied, her chin lifted with defensiveness. "And it really doesn't matter where I've been, I'm here now."

"Where's Rebecca? Where's my baby?" Ruth asked, her voice as demanding as her husband's.

"She isn't with me. She's playing with friends."

"How dare you take her and disappear. We've been frantic with worry," Ruth exclaimed.

"And how dare you try to twist her mind against me," Alicia replied angrily. "How dare you tell her I'm a bad person and she should forget all about me."

Ruth flushed and stepped closer to her husband.

"Now, now. Let's settle down a bit." Broderick forced a laugh. "Goodness, it's too damned early in the morning to get all worked up." He gestured to the sofa. "Please…let's be rational and sit down and discuss the situation."

Cameron walked over to the sofa and sat next to Alicia, fighting the impulse to take one of her hands in his, present a united front to this man and woman who'd frightened her so much she'd lived a life on the run.

Ruth sank down in one of the wing-backed chairs, her gaze fluttering from wall to wall, but never landing on Alicia or Cameron. Broderick stood at the back of her chair. "Can we offer you some juice…a cup of coffee?" he asked.

Alicia shook her head curtly. "This isn't a social call, Broderick. I'm here to discuss Rebecca's future."

"We all want what's best for Robert's little girl," he replied.

Cameron saw Alicia's growing tension in the way her hands clasped her purse handle so tight her knuckles grew white. "If you truly want what's best for Rebecca, then you'll leave us alone, leave her alone."

"That's not acceptable," Broderick stated flatly. "We can do for Rebecca what you can't. We can raise her in a proper home, with the best schools. Robert would have wanted that."

"No. Robert wanted to get away from you," Alicia's voice rose with anger and pain. "You destroyed Robert, and I won't let you do the same to Rebecca.''

Broderick's eyes narrowed and Cameron's adrenaline rose in response to the implied threat. ''Be careful, girlie. I make a powerful enemy. I've already got the paperwork drawn up seeking full custody of Rebecca. If you don't want to settle this outside of court, we'll settle it in court and I know you don't have the funds for a court battle.''

''Oh, but I do.'' Alicia's chin went up a notch. ''Cameron has been kind enough to loan me enough money for a defense fund.''

Broderick snorted derisively. ''I should have known a gold digger like you would find another sap. How many times did you sleep with him before he offered you money?''

Cameron heard Alicia's swift intake of breath. The implication of Broderick's words was ugly…and Cameron couldn't allow him to talk to Alicia that way. ''Be careful, Mr. Randall. I make a very powerful enemy,'' he said softly, throwing the man's words back at him.

''It doesn't matter anyway. It's not going to come to a court battle,'' Alicia said. With hands that trembled, she opened her purse and drew out some papers. ''I found some interesting things in Robert's briefcase last night.''

Broderick frowned and Ruth nervously fumbled with her pearls. ''I can't imagine what Robert would have in his briefcase that has anything to do with Rebecca and our rights as grandparents to protect her from a whoring, alcoholic, abusive mother.''

Cameron rose to his feet, the blood pounding in his temples. Alicia grabbed his arm. "It's all right, Cameron. He can't hurt me with his words," she said. "They are no longer in control." Cameron looked at her, saw the strength radiating in her gaze, and sank back down.

Alicia focused her gaze back on her in-laws. "Do you remember a man named Henry Brockburn? Dr. Henry Brockburn?"

Broderick blanched and Ruth gasped. Cameron had no idea what the man meant to them, but it was obvious he meant something unpleasant. "I...I don't know what you're talking about," Broderick blustered.

"Oh, I think you do," Alicia countered. "The man was put in prison years ago for selling babies. He sold you a baby. A little boy named Robert born to Mary Kimble, father unknown."

"Damn you," Broderick took a step forward and again Cameron stood. This time Alicia didn't place a restraining hand on him, instead she stood next to him.

"No, damn you!" she exclaimed. "Robert wasn't your son, and that means Rebecca isn't your granddaughter. There are no blood ties between you and what you did years ago was illegal. Want to take me to court? Take me. I'll hold press conferences, I'll tell the world that the great, powerful Randalls illegally bought a baby boy, then proceeded to destroy that baby's life through control and manipulation."

Broderick sputtered wordlessly, but Cameron

could tell by the defeat in his eyes that Alicia had won. "What do you want?" the man asked. "How much money do I have to pay to keep your mouth shut?"

Alicia's gaze held no triumph, but only a deep sadness. "I don't want your money. I don't want anything from you except to be left alone to raise my daughter. That's what Robert would have wanted."

Broderick nodded and Ruth got up and left the room. "You win," Broderick said. "But it was a dirty fight."

Alicia smiled tightly. "You taught me everything I know." She grabbed Cameron's arm, her finger-nails digging into his arm. "Come on, we're fin-ished. Let's get out of here."

They didn't speak until they were out of the house and in the car. Then, Alicia turned to him, her eyes shining with excitement. "I did it," she exclaimed with utter joy. "Finally, it's over." Tears of hap-piness sparkled like diamonds on her lashes. "Re-becca and I can go anywhere we want and not look over our shoulders. We can start a new life."

Cameron nodded slowly, happy for her. Now the only thing to find out was if there was any room in her new life for him.

Chapter 15

"So, what are your plans now?" Cameron asked.

Alicia started the car and backed out of the driveway. She wanted to get as far away from this house as quickly as possible. "My only plan at this moment is to go pick up Rebecca from the day care. But first I want to stop by my house and get your check." She smiled at him gratefully. "I don't think I'll be needing it."

"I'm glad things are working out the way you wanted."

"I knew something was going on with Robert in the weeks before his death. He was more optimistic, was making plans for the three of us to move. Thank heavens I found those papers in his briefcase." She pulled into the driveway of the house she'd shared with Robert.

"Nice place," Cameron observed. "Won't you miss this?"

Alicia stared at the house where she'd lived for her married life. "Yes, it's a nice house, but I won't miss anything about it." And she knew the truth of her statement. "It never felt like home, never felt like it really belonged to me." She couldn't tell him she'd felt more at home in his house, with its scuffed walls and antiquated plumbing. "Come on in and I'll get you the check."

He followed her inside. She took him through the living room and into the kitchen where she opened a drawer and pulled out the check.

She clutched it for a moment, realizing it was the last link to him. After she returned it there would be no more reason for her to contact him, no more reason to have anything to do with him.

She turned around and held it out to him. He tossed his hat on the table, then stepped closer to her. He took the check and shoved it into his pocket.

"Well...I guess that's that," she said, wishing he'd move away from her...come closer to her...love her. How she wished he'd love her.

He reached out and stroked a strand of her hair away from her face. She flinched at his touch. How could he not see that him standing so near, touching her in the most innocent manner tortured her?

"Now that you're truly free, I guess there's a world of options open to you."

She nodded and stared at the floor, unable to look at him.

"Is returning to Mustang one of those options?"

His voice sounded curiously strained and when Alicia looked up, she met his intense gaze.

"I...there's nothing there for me." Her reply was faint as she felt herself falling into the depths of his eyes.

"You made a lot of friends there. You've already begun to build a life for you and Rebecca in Mustang."

She nodded, unwilling to tell him the reason why she'd never consider living in Mustang again. She couldn't, not loving him the way she did.

"I'm there," he added.

The words rang in the stillness of the kitchen and reverberated in Alicia's head. She didn't know what to make of them, what he meant? She opened her mouth to speak, but no words would come.

He raked a hand through his hair, his gaze still locked on her. "Samuel caught up with me yesterday afternoon. Funny, I thought he'd come to kill me and he came for forgiveness." He looked over his shoulder, out the window, obviously momentarily lost in thought. "I didn't realize until talking with him how much I'd allowed my hurt...my anger to color everything in my life. And the funny thing is, I didn't even love Ginny...not really...not the way a man should love the woman he intends to spend the rest of his life with."

Cameron focused his gaze back on her. "Ginny wanted marriage, and I wasn't ready to commit. She found what she was looking for in Samuel's arms, in his heart and now I can be glad for them. I know now why I wasn't willing to commit to her. She wasn't my soul mate, she didn't own any pieces of my heart.''

Alicia's breath felt trapped in her chest as she saw the light that shone in his eyes. She was afraid to breathe, afraid to move...afraid that somehow that light might disappear.

He stepped closer to her, bringing with him the scent that was intrinsically his own. Placing his hands on her shoulders, he kept his gaze locked with hers. ''I had to face all that baggage with Samuel in order to free my heart and realize I found my soul mate. You, Alicia...you're my soul mate, the woman I want to spend the rest of my life with.''

His words soared through Alicia, filling her up with euphoria. He loves me, her heart sang. Cameron Gallagher loves me. Tears spilled from her eyes, unexpected but joyous. ''Oh Cameron. I do so love you,'' she whispered. She could say no more, for her lips were captured by his as he wrapped her in his embrace.

His mouth moved against hers with hunger as his hands stroked up and down her back. It was as if he couldn't get close enough, couldn't hold her tight enough, couldn't kiss her deeply enough to satisfy him.

She felt the same way. She wanted to crawl inside him, wrap him around her, wear him like a second skin for the rest of her life.

''Come back to Mustang,'' he murmured against her neck when he broke the kiss. ''Come back home and be my wife, my love.''

''Yes. I can't think of anywhere I'd rather be.''

He framed her face with his hands, gazing deeply into her eyes. "Be sure, Alicia. You thought you loved me when you were afraid and on the run. You aren't running any longer and I need to know that you are absolutely certain of your love for me."

She looked at him, loving him with every fiber of her being. "The only place I intend running to from now on is into your arms as often as possible. I love you, Cameron, and I'm through running away. I want to build a life with you, a life filled with love and laughter."

"I want that, too." His eyes flamed with emotion and again his lips sought hers, hungrily possessing hers. Alicia knew there would never be another man for her, another love like theirs. The warmth of their love filled the corners of her heart.

"I hope you don't want a long engagement," he said when the kiss had ended. "I want you as my wife as soon as possible."

"I've always thought long engagements were silly," she agreed. She moaned as his mouth moved down her neck, trailing heat with every kiss. "Cameron, I have to go get Rebecca," she finally managed to say. "I promised her she wouldn't be at the day-care place for very long."

"I have a feeling this won't take long," he said, his eyes gleaming wickedly. Alicia smiled, and gave into his caresses, his sweet love.

Forty-five minutes later Alicia and Cameron pulled up in front of the day-care center and Alicia went inside to get Rebecca.

"Mommy!" Rebecca greeted her with a hug and a kiss. "I'm so happy to see you."

Alicia laughed. "And I'm so happy to see you." She pulled Rebecca to her, held her for a long moment as she thanked the stars above that the nightmare was over. Never again would she have to worry about somebody taking Rebecca away from her. "Guess what?" she said as she released her daughter.

"What?"

"I have a surprise out in the car for you."

Rebecca's eyes widened. "A surprise? Is it a new toy?"

"Something better," Alicia said.

"A pony?"

Alicia laughed. "Something even better than a pony."

"Better than a pony?" Rebecca drew a deep breath. "I'm out of guesses."

"Then you'd better go see what it is," Alicia replied.

She followed Rebecca out the day-care door. As they left the building, Cameron climbed out of the car.

"Mr. Lallager!" Rebecca squealed in delight and tore off toward him as fast as her little legs would carry her.

Alicia's heart threatened to burst with happiness as she watched the man she loved scoop up the little girl she loved in his arms.

Rebecca wound her arms around Cameron's neck

and hugged him tight. "Oh, I hoped and hoped I'd see you again."

Cameron closed his eyes and returned the hug. "I had my fingers crossed that I'd see you again."

Rebecca smiled in delight. "You did? I did, too!" Cameron laughed, his laughter mingling with Alicia's and Rebecca grinned, obviously not getting the joke, but happy just the same.

"How would you like to come back to Mustang and live with me forever and ever?" Cameron asked the little girl.

She frowned. "With Mommy?"

Cameron's gaze warmed Alicia from head to toes. "Oh yes, definitely with your mommy."

"Then the answer is yes!" Rebecca exclaimed with excitement. Her excitement ebbed and she looked at her mother uncertainly. "But what about the people monsters…will they find us?"

"You don't have to worry about the people monsters any more," Cameron said.

Alicia knelt down next to her daughter. "Mr. Gallagher and I are going to get married. That will make the three of us a real family and people monsters don't bother with real families."

Rebecca nodded slowly, her brow furrowed in a thoughtful frown. "So that means I'll have two daddies. My daddy in Heaven and Mr. Lallager can be my daddy here, right?"

Again Alicia's heart swelled as Cameron drew Rebecca back into the circle of his arms. "That's right, sweetheart. I'll be your daddy here."

Rebecca placed a little hand on the side of Cameron's face, a huge smile on her face. "Oh boy. I'm so lucky. I get a real cowboy for a daddy."

Cameron laughed, for the first time truly proud of his old nickname. "I'm so lucky," he returned. "I get a real cowgirl for a daughter." His gaze turned to Alicia. "And the woman of my dreams for my wife. How lucky can one cowboy get?"

Alicia gazed at this man...this cowboy who had stolen her heart and claimed it as his own. She knew the sweetness of his kisses, the magic of his touch, but most of all, she knew that in his love...she was home.

Epilogue

"I've never seen a man so impatient," Elena Richards said as she flew through the bedroom door and quickly closed it behind her. "Cameron actually told everyone to sit down and be quiet so he could make you his bride."

Alicia laughed, unsurprised by Cameron's actions. Despite the fact that Elena and Alicia had pulled together a wedding in less than two weeks, it hadn't been fast enough for Cameron, who acted as if at any moment Alicia might suddenly disappear.

"Oh honey...you look gorgeous," Elena exclaimed.

"Are you sure it's okay?" Alicia whirled around to view her reflection in the dresser mirror. She smiled self-consciously and ran a hand down the satin skirt of the ivory gown. "I know it's crazy to wear a traditional gown…I mean, I've been married before, and I have a daughter…''

"Stop," Elena commanded. "You look beautiful, and you and Cameron both wanted the traditional trappings."

"The first time I got married it felt all wrong. I was dressed in my waitress uniform and neither of us knew the two witnesses."

"And how does it feel this time?" Elena asked softly.

Alicia turned toward her and smiled. "So right it's almost frightening."

Elena laughed. "That's because it is right. I've never seen two people more suited to one another than you and Cameron." She leaned forward and kissed Alicia on the cheek. "And I don't know any-one else I'd rather have as a sister."

Alicia hugged Elena. In the past several weeks the two women had developed the beginnings of what Alicia knew would be a strong, lasting friend-ship.

"Mommy?" Rebecca entered the room and stopped short. "Oh Mommy, you look like a fairy princess," she exclaimed.

"And you look quite lovely yourself," Alicia re-plied. Rebecca wore a frilly dress, the blue an exact match for her eyes. On her feet were the beloved red cowboy boots.

"Daddy Lallager says hurry up. He can't wait anymore." Without waiting for a reply, Rebecca turned and whirled out of the room.

Alicia tried to still the frantic pounding of her

heart as she left the bedroom and walked into the living room. The furniture had been taken out, replaced by folding chairs and every chair was occupied by the friends and acquaintances Alicia had made in Mustang.

But she didn't notice the people in the chairs. Her gaze was fixed solely on the man who stood next to the preacher.

Cameron. He looked so tall, so handsome and his eyes flamed with the fires Alicia knew would warm her not only through the long winter ahead but all the winters of their lives.

As the preacher began the ceremony, Rebecca tugged on Alicia's skirt. "Mommy?" she said in an exaggerated whisper. "Mommy, it's really, really important."

Alicia smiled an embarrassed apology to the preacher and to Cameron. Soft laughter rose from the amused audience behind them. "What, honey?" Alicia asked.

"I got my fingers double, double crossed for a baby sister," Rebecca exclaimed.

As the people in the chairs laughed, Cameron picked Rebecca up in his arms. "That's funny. I've got my fingers double, double crossed for the same thing," he said.

"Really and truly?" Rebecca asked.

He nodded, eyes twinkling. "Cross my cowboy heart," he said.

Rebecca turned to the people behind them. "And cowboys never lie," she announced.

Amid the laughter, witnessed by friends, Alicia

and Cameron said the vows that would bind them together forever. As the preacher proclaimed them man and wife and Cameron's lips claimed hers in a fiery kiss filled with promise and love, Alicia knew she would never run again.

She was finally home.

* * * * *

Don't miss the next exciting story
in the MUSTANG, MONTANA *miniseries*
featuring Johnny Crockett
and his unexpected homecoming…
coming in June 1998,
only from Silhouette Intimate Moments.

COMING NEXT MONTH